The Devil's Inn

DAVID WATKINS

For Mum and Dad
You probably won't like this one.

Part One: Arrivals

"We can't stop here. This is a back road somewhere on the way to the middle of nowhere."

Chapter 1

On the day that Mark killed a man for the first – but not the last - time, he ended up being late to pick up his girlfriend. Screeching to a halt outside her flat, he jumped out. She was sat on the outside wall, a grin lighting up her face.

"Hey, you," Elana said.

"Sorry, traffic was an arse."

She slipped off her coat: a thick plain jumper and jeans hiding her figure. Mark held the door to the car open for her and got a smile for his troubles. Climbing in himself, he gunned the engine. The stereo blared out Counting Crows *'Mr Jones'* and he turned it down quickly.

"Did you have it that loud on the way over?" Elana asked. The set of her mouth showed, despite the earlier smile, she was still annoyed about James.

"Nah," Mark lied, "but as soon as that tune came on I had to turn it up."

"It is a great song."

And, like that, the tension between them eased. Mark pulled into the slow moving traffic and took the first road from Richmond signposted to Kingston.

"You weren't joking about him then."

"No," Mark said. "He sounded really down on the phone. I couldn't just leave him for the weekend."

"You could."

"You don't mean that. Come on, he was depressed."

She snorted a laugh at him. "James? Depressed? That implies he has feelings."

"Well, he might have had for this one. I think he really loved her." Mark paused long enough to swear at the traffic. "He *is* one of my best mates."

"Such a good mate you can't remember her name."

"Susan," Mark said in a flash.

"Sharon."

"Dammit, I was close." Mark grinned at her. "Come on, it's a party. You won't even have to talk to him much."

"Apart from the three hour drive."

"Well, apart from that, yes."

"Are you sure he's invited?"

"He knows tons of people there."

"That's not the same as invited, Mark," she sighed. "I know why he wasn't invited: because he's a cock."

"He's not that bad."

She didn't answer and lost herself in the music until they pulled up outside James's flat half an hour later. Another suburban street. *I cannot wait to leave this shit-hole.* Elana sighed again as Mark parked.

James was sat on his bag looking dejected until the car pulled up alongside him. He was wearing a thin jacket that hung well on his broad shoulders. An Oxford check shirt, jeans and expensive looking shoes completed his outfit. His hair looked like he had come from a salon and his skin had a light tan to it.

And that's the problem, he's good looking and knows it. This is going to be a long drive. Elana stared down the street. Non-descript houses, long ago split into flats, lined a featureless road. Cars filled the sides of the street, artificially narrowing it. At the moment, the cars belonged to commuters, parking as close to the train station as they could without paying. Tonight, those cars would go and be replaced by the residents of the identikit houses. *It's like Hell on Earth.*

James looked confused until Mark got out, then his face creased into a big grin. The two men embraced like they hadn't seen each other for years. Mark touched the hem of James' coat.

"You know it's, like, January, right?"

"Nice wheels," James said, ignoring him.

"Yep. Got my bonus. I've always wanted one."

"You've always wanted an Audi A6?" James moved round to the boot, which opened automatically. Mark's grin became wider.

"It's a brilliant car."

"Yeah, sweet," James said, opening the rear door of the car. "Seriously though, you've *always* wanted an A6?"

4

Mark got in behind the wheel again, and both doors slammed in unison. "Yep."

"Seriously nice leather." James looked impressed for the first time. "Hi Elana, how's things?"

"Fine," she said. She tried to smile at him, but the corners of her mouth barely made it above the horizontal.

"Nice jumper."

"Is everybody in?" Mark intoned in his best Jim Morrison voice.

"Ramblers, let's get rambling," James quoted Quentin Tarantino. "Seriously, what does that mean anyway? That's got to be one of his worst ever lines. "

"I like it," Elana said. *Seriously, seriously, seriously. James was in serious need of a thesaurus.*

"Great film," Mark said.

"His best," James agreed.

Mark eased the car back onto the road and they were on their way.

"Nice sound," James said as they joined the motorway, heading south. Almost immediately, the traffic slowed to a crawl.

"It's Bose," Mark said. The smugness in his voice was almost a physical presence.

"Got one of them at home. Not that impressed really. For six hundred notes I was expecting more."

"Buy some cotton buds," Mark said. "Bose is brilliant."

"If I bought cotton buds, I'd stick them in my ears so I wouldn't have to listen to this shit. How do you put up with this Els?"

Elana rolled her eyes. James had not stopped talking since getting in the car. "I like it."

"Who is this whiny old twat anyway?"

"Ryan Adams," Mark said.

"Bryan Adams? Jesus, is he still alive?"

"No, Ryan Adams. Americana."

"American't more like. Seriously though, this is shit. What else you got?"

"New one by Elbow," Elana said, picking up a CD at random.

"Now, that's more like it. Proper British misery," James said. "Stick it on Els."

5

She did as asked and carefully put the Ryan Adams CD back in its case. With any luck, James would sleep soon and she could put it back on. She gazed out the window at the world not rushing by.

"What's with this traffic?" she said.

"Relax, it's just the junction for the M25," Mark said, squeezing her thigh.

"Is it going to be like this all the way to Devon?" James asked.

"Nah, we'll be fine when we get past the next junction. It's always like this on a Friday." Mark started tapping the wheel in time with the music.

"Really?" James said. "How do you know? You been down recently?"

"Yeah, we went a couple of weekends ago."

"Did you see him then?"

"Yep."

"Christ, why are you going again so soon?"

"Mate, he's thirty, he's having a party."

"Pasty is always having a party."

Mark chuckled at that. "Yeah, any excuse."

"If he's thirty, isn't it about time you stopped calling him Pasty?" Elana said. They'd visited Tom a couple of weeks ago and once she'd got used to his accent, she had found him very funny. There had been a couple of moments where he'd been staring at her, and the looks filled her with dread. *He couldn't recognise her surely?*

Mark and James shared a glance in the rear view mirror. "Nah!" they said at the same time.

"But he's not even from Cornwall."

"That's what makes it funny." Mark said.

"It's irony see? He's from Devon, so it's going to piss him off," James said. "Same as Geordie. He's from Leeds."

Mark was right. As soon as they passed the junction for the M25, the traffic eased and they were in the clear. Without really trying, Mark hit one hundred before slowing to a more respectable eighty, the smug grin returning to his face.

James went to sleep, which instantly made Elana relax. She smiled at Mark as they moved onto the A303. "Love you."

"Love you too." He took his eyes off the road for a second and returned her smile.

"Are we going to stop for some lunch?" She rubbed her stomach. "I'm so bored, all I can think about is eating."

"There's services up ahead, the new ones."

"Terrific."

They pulled into the car park of the services a couple of minutes later. As soon as the handbrake was on, Mark turned and shouted 'bang' in James's face. James sat bolt upright, a cry escaping his lips.

"Don't be a dick, man." James shook his head and rubbed his eyes.

As soon as they were out of the car, Mark said, "Watch this."

He raised his hand with a solemn expression on his face. The boot swung open.

"Nice," James said.

"Yeah, I used the Force. Look," Mark lowered his hand and the boot slowly closed in time with his action.

"I don't know what's worse: that you've clearly practised that or that you think I don't know you're pressing a button on your key in your other hand." James shook his head.

"Rumbled," Elana said.

"Oh come on, it's cool."

"It's alright. It is a nice car," James said. "But seriously, you've always wanted an A6?"

"Yes."

"Have you heard of a little company called Porsche? Mercedes?"

"Grub up," Mark said with a laugh. He held Elana's hand as they crossed the car park, deliberately waiting until they were across the car park before pressing the 'lock car' button on his key. The A6 replied with a beep. Elana slapped his arm playfully.

"Stop being an arsehole."

They ate in Pizza Hut. Mark ordered spicy, James pepperoni and Elana vegetarian. She ignored James's comment about being a 'vagitarian', although she was disappointed to see Mark laugh. Both of the men piled their salads high and ordered a beer.

Twenty minutes later, they left Pizza Hut stuffed and happy. As they got close to the car, James shouted "Shotgun!" and jumped into the front seat.

"Dude, get out of the car."

7

"What?" James looked genuinely hurt. "I called it fair and square."

"Come on, man, we're not eighteen anymore."

"Well, you're clearly not with all that grey and those lines."

"I look distinguished and they are laughter lines."

"Keep telling yourself that, pal. Grey at thirty, it's a sad thing to behold."

"It's ok," Elana said. "I'm exhausted, so I'll have a kip. You two can wind each other up about music." She kissed Mark on the cheek and got in the back of the car.

"Yes, Elana," James smiled. "I like to see people who appreciate the sanctity of shotgun being called."

Mark rolled his eyes. It was at least another two hours to Huntleigh according to the SatNav: it was going to seem like longer.

Elana sank into the leather seats, resting her head on the window. The leather bothered her, of course, but she couldn't deny how comfortable the seats were. Mark was so pleased with the car, and she had to admit that it had been a good purchase. Still, a hell of a lot of money, though.

We could have bought a house together with the money as deposit. A nice two bed house, somewhere like Exeter or even Plymouth. Maybe with a garden, but definitely with a spare room.

She rested her hand on her full stomach and fell into a deep, dreamless sleep.

Elana awoke an hour later, groggy and disorientated. Her neck ached and her legs were numb. She tried to stretch, but ended up rubbing her neck on the seatbelt.

"I thought these cars were meant to be comfortable," she moaned.

"It is," Mark said. "Hiya gorgeous."

"Not feeling gorgeous. Where are we?"

"Just past Exeter. Turning onto the A38," Mark said in his best West Country accent.

"Where the hell are you supposed to be from? India?"

"The A38?" Elana asked.

"Yep," James turned to look at her. "Just an hour to go. We made good time whilst you were asleep. Can we turn the music up now?" He directed the question at Mark.

"Let her wake up a bit man."

"Is this Iron Maiden?" Elana asked.

"Oh yes!" James said.

"Just a trip down memory lane, babe. We'll change it."

"Not till 'Run to the hills,'" James said. He reached to turn the volume up, but Mark used the steering controls to quieten it.

"Just leave it."

"You've got a Bose stereo, playing the greatest British rock band of all time, quietly," James raised his eyebrows at Mark. "Seriously, what is wrong with you?"

"Led Zeppelin," Elana said.

"What?"

"Led Zep are the greatest British rock band of all time."

Mark laughed. "She's got you there mate."

"No," James said. "They're the greatest rock band. Iron Maiden are the greatest British rock band."

"Led Zep are British, you tw-" Mark stopped himself. "-idiot."

"Yes, but they're so great, they have their own category."

And so it went, James trying hard to defend his viewpoint with increasingly more ludicrous claims. Elana looked out of the window and tuned him out. The road ahead split and they took the A38 turning. Something didn't feel right, but Elana couldn't place it. *Still feel lousy from the sleep, afternoon kips always leave me feeling rubbish.*

"Yes!" James shouted and turned up the stereo. He began to sing, loudly and badly. Mark started to laugh and joined in, equally badly. They mangled all the words except the chorus, although, to be fair, that was the easy bit.

Elana smiled, feeling the tension of the city draining away as more greenery came into view. *Maybe this will be a good weekend after all.*

Bored, as James had changed Iron Maiden into Muse and the noise was now worse, Elana picked up a map and flicked to Devon. The green expanse of Dartmoor covered most of the page. She traced her finger round the edge, then went up a bit and found Huntleigh.

Up.

She found Exeter quickly and the A38.

Up from Dartmoor.

"Guys, why are we on the A38? We should be on the A30."

"Got a SatNav, babe," Mark said, tapping the screen.

"Yeah, where we're going we don't need maps," James said, trying and failing to sound like Christopher Lloyd in 'Back To The Future'.

She sat forward on the seat, seatbelt gently tugging back on her shoulder. "According to this, Huntleigh is north of Dartmoor. We're now south."

"You must be reading it wrong. SatNav said come this way," Mark said, shaking his head slightly.

"Trust the technology," James said.

"Look, I can read a bloody map. We're on the wrong road."

"Which way did you come last time?" James asked.

"Can't remember," Mark said. Doubt had crept into his voice. "Didn't have this car then, didn't use SatNav."

"No, we used a map," Elana said with a sigh. "We're on the wrong road."

On cue, the SatNav said: "At the next junction turn left." The screen said five hundred metres and an arrow pointing left. Elana looked over the map.

"That'll take us up onto Dartmoor."

"Yeah, but is it right?"

"Yes," she said after a pause. She was trying to quickly trace a path from the A38 to Huntleigh. The lines on the map were very small compared to the thick green and yellow line that indicated their current road. "But we'll go over the moor. Might take a while."

"We're in no rush," Mark said. "That's why we all took the day off remember?"

"Yeah," James grumbled, "but I thought we'd be in a pub for most of the day, not your stupid boring car."

"It's not a boring car," Mark said, indicating to come off at the slip road. "It's just got shit SatNav."

"Maybe we should come back on, and go round," Elana suggested.

"Nah," Mark said. "That'll take just as long as this way. Besides, I'm bored of dual carriageway. It'll be fun to go cross country."

"Where's your sense of adventure?" James grinned at her, and she got a glimpse of the good looking man she'd first bumped into at university. *Long time ago.*

Once off the dual carriageway, Mark followed the signs to Buckfastleigh then Princetown. Soon, they passed a sign saying "Welcome to Dartmoor. Please drive with moor care."

"Moor care," Mark sniggered. "I like that."

The blue skies were beginning to darken as the sun was slowly sinking below the horizon. On the screen in the middle of the dashboard was an external temperature gauge. It hadn't risen above five degrees centigrade the entire journey. Now it sank below zero with a beep.

"Slow down Mark," Elana said with a shiver. Her bad feeling was back. Her legs felt tense, like she was ready to run. Despite the cold outside, a single bead of sweat ran down her back. "Maybe we should just go back on the dual carriageway," she muttered.

"Say something?" Mark asked, catching her eyes in the mirror.

She shook her head and resumed looking out of the window. All she could see for miles was the utter bleakness of Dartmoor.

Chapter 2

Jeff McCarthy had had enough. His feet ached; his back felt like it was about to spasm and there was enough sweat on his back for him to worry about it freezing as the temperature dropped. He would give anything to be sat at home, by a roaring fire with a whiskey in hand, reading a book instead. Any book: it wouldn't even have to be a good one. His walking boots were rubbing his ankles and he was pretty sure he had a blister the size of a golf ball on his right foot. *So much for the expensive hiking socks.*

Sandra was, of course, loving every minute of it.

She wasn't looking at him, she was scanning the horizon, with a huge grin on her face as the wind blew her blonde hair back. She looked like someone from the front of those SAGA magazines. She had kept her figure and looks as he had lost hair and gained weight. It had been her idea to start walking; her idea for them to spend some 'quality time' together.

So far, the quality time had involved the pain in his feet and back and the coldest wind Jeff had ever experienced. His lips felt chapped and he knew his cheeks were glowing bright red (although, if he were honest, that wasn't entirely down to the cold).

"It's fantastic here isn't it?" Sandra said, for the tenth time that afternoon.

"Yes dear," Jeff said. He took a big swig of water from his cantina and stood up, feeling the weight of his pack across his shoulders and in the small of his back. He tried to suppress a grunt, but judging by Sandra's concerned look he failed.

"We haven't even walked that far," she said, but not unkindly.

"I know," Jeff said, "it just feels like it."

"You wanted to do the Lyke Wake walk."

Yes, but not today. We've got months before we do that, we should be building up slowly. Instead of complaining he said, "How much further till the pub?"

Sandra looked at the map. "Not far, another two miles maybe. We'll be there in-" she stopped and took in Jeff's demeanour, "-about an hour. Maybe forty five minutes." She flashed him the smile that had turned his head all those years ago. "Think of the pint you've earned!"

"One?"

He started walking, looking at the compass heading on his GPS. It was bright grey, with a large colour screen. It still had the sheen of a new toy. Jeff loved his gadgets, but had been a little dismayed to open this one on Christmas morning. It had told him that Sandra was serious about doing more walking in the New Year.

He had pretended to be pleased; it wasn't worth a fight.

Jeff blamed the walking society that she had joined last summer. In six months she had turned from a stay at home slob like himself to talking about bagging Munros and doing this stupid Lyke Wake walk in the summer. She had even mentioned the Three Peak Challenge for the following summer. He didn't know what that entailed, but one peak didn't sound good, so three sounded horrendous. How had she succeeded in persuading him to join in?

Easy, really: it was that or split up.

Jeff did not fancy being single again. The thought of going on a date terrified him, but not as much as the quality of who would go on a date with him now? He would not get a woman of the calibre of Sandra anymore, no way. One look at his fat bald head and any good looking woman would run a mile.

"Do you need help with that?" Sandra asked as he adjusted the straps on his pack.

"No, I'm ok," he said, then added "thanks" almost as an afterthought. *It's not that heavy.* It had a waterproof overcoat – one of those thin ones designed to go over whatever you're wearing and that you have no chance of getting back in the bag once it's out; his water bottle, now over half empty; a spare pair of socks, although he had no idea why, and some food and snacks. He was embarrassed that the bag was digging into his shoulders, despite being light.

"Not far now, hon," Sandra said. She was weaving her way through the gorse bushes and bracken like she had been here every day of her life. Her boots looked well worn, despite being six months old.

Thick socks could be seen under her walking trousers and her coat fitted snugly despite being extremely warm. Her own pack seemed to float on her back.

Jeff took in his surroundings again. Hills rolled away in every direction, with the odd rocky tor breaking the monotony of the view. An occasional wild pony would show a little interest in them before resuming munching on the grass. Sheep herded together in the distance, but none came close to the path they were walking on. He hadn't seen anywhere so desolate in his entire life – and he had grown up within spitting distance of the Brecon Beacons.

Dartmoor was probably the bleakest place he had ever seen.

In the distance he saw a solid line of white cloud descend and touch the tip of the nearest hill. It looked like someone had thrown a blanket over the summit as he watched.

"What's that?"

"Relax, it's just low cloud," Sandra said. "The weather changes up here very quickly."

"Do we turn back?"

"Don't be daft. It's eight miles back to the car. That cloud could roll right over us."

"We seem to be heading straight at it."

"No, we'll be going off to the left. See those rocks there? That's where we're heading."

Jeff followed her point, but couldn't see how those rocks looked different to any other rocks they had passed so far. *How can she tell where they were going?* Instead of arguing, he grunted.

She smiled at him. "Don't worry. We'll be in the pub in no time. We'll have some early dinner and then get a taxi or bus back to the car. Ok?"

It was the best thing he had heard all day.

Sandra watched Jeff slump his way towards her and tried hard to hide her disappointment. The wind blew her hair back from her face again and she shivered as the cold caressed her cheeks. She turned away from him and scanned the horizon. The bank of cloud seemed to be spreading, but quite slowly. She had never seen anything like it before, but then she'd only been walking for just over half a year. Friends had told her about the mists on Dartmoor; how they suddenly came and if you weren't careful you'd get very, very lost. There was a phrase for it, but she couldn't remember it just now.

She wasn't worried about the mist. Their route would take them round it and they didn't have far to go now before they reached the pub. *Just keep an eye on it and don't tell Jeff.*

He'll only moan some more.

Why did he agree to this? She threw him an encouraging smile as they walked down the narrow track. He was looking at the GPS rather than where he was going; probably counting down the yards to the pub. If he wasn't careful, he'd trip and twist his ankle or worse.

"What's that?" Jeff asked again. She looked where he was pointing and saw a dark smudge on the horizon, near to the wall of cloud.

"Not sure." She squinted, but the smudge remained a dark blob. She made a mental note to make that optician's appointment when they got home and lifted her binoculars. She was surprised to see the figure of a person swim into focus.

He or she was wearing a long brown overcoat, tied at the waist and with a hood obscuring his or her face. He appeared to be standing still on the edge of the mist and he was looking right at her. She wasn't sure how she knew that, but the thought made her drop the binoculars.

"Careful!" Jeff said.

"Sorry." She bent to pick them up and when she returned her gaze to the spot, the man had gone. "Where'd he go?"

"Who?"

"The man on the hill over there. Where'd he go?" Sandra looked at the hill. There were no bushes, no drops and no small mounds. The man had just disappeared.

"Who cares?" Jeff muttered. "Just another walking nut. He's closer to the pub though."

"Give it a rest about the pub Jeff," Sandra snapped. "It was a monk. He was looking right at me."

"Of course he was. There's no-one else up here for miles is there."

Goosebumps raised along her arms. Where had the man gone? Had he walked deliberately into the fog? The idea was absurd: it was dangerous on Dartmoor unless you took care. Moor care as it said on all the signs in the car parks. No-one would actually walk into the mist if they didn't have to, surely?

"Come on, let's go," Jeff said and he resumed walking down the path, heading for the rocks that were their marker. He stopped after about fifty yards, "You coming?"

"I'm coming." Another thing bothered her about the man on the hill. He'd clearly been wearing a monks outfit, and he had definitely deliberately hidden his face. *Come on now, its cold out here, maybe he was trying to keep warm.*

Maybe.

She lifted her map to look at it, even though she knew that what she was searching for would not be there. The map was folded to show the area they were in, snug in its waterproof case. She traced the path they were on, confirmed the bearing was correct and then scanned the surrounding area.

There were no monasteries marked on the map.

Chapter 3

A tractor caused them to slow right down before they got anywhere near Princetown; a large trailer full of manure made it nigh on impossible to overtake at any point on the winding road. The manure would occasionally blow out of the back of the trailer and splash onto the car.

Elana didn't need to see his face to know that Mark was getting annoyed.

"Turn left just here," she said. Mark yanked the wheel hard to the left and they turned onto a narrow lane. High hedges lined the road, which had enough mud on it to count as a dirt track rather than road, but at least the tractor wasn't slowing them down. Mark pushed the accelerator down and grinned as the engine roared in response. Winding across the moor for about a mile, they then came to a T-junction onto the main road.

"Left," James said, pointing at the SatNav. He proceeded to rummage through the CD case again and his eyes lit up on seeing something. He pulled out Led Zeppelin Remasters. "Now we're talking."

Elana looked down at the map, just as they passed a sign saying Yelverton. *That's not right.* She spun her head to look at the corresponding sign on the other side of the road.

"Wait!" she called, "Princetown's the other way. We're going the wrong way."

"Fucking useless piece of shit!" Mark roared, slapping the SatNav screen. "You are going back on Monday."

He turned into a lay-by and pulled up, tugging the handbrake before they'd fully stopped causing a slight skid.

"What're we stopping for?" James asked.

"Need a piss." Mark slammed the door hard enough to make the car shake.

"Wow," James said, grinning at Elana. "Must be his time of the month."

She rolled her eyes and got out the car.

"Hey! Do you mind?" Mark said and he crossed to the other side of the road. A thick gorse bush sat on the edge of the road, as big a public toilet as he'd ever seen. He walked around it until the view of the road was obscured enough for him to feel comfortable.

Elana tutted and turned away from Mark. She didn't know if it was endearing or annoying that Mark refused to relieve himself in front of her. *Sweet probably.* She had been with people that would happily do a lot worse.

"It's beautiful," Elana muttered to herself, looking around the bleak moor. Wind whistled through the long grass, and in the distance the clouds hung heavy, topping the hills with grey woollen hats. There were no lights or any other moving object for miles in any direction.

She took out her phone and switched the camera on, turning it into panoramic mode. She swept the camera from left to right, keeping the indicator in the right zone to complete the photograph. It was a neat feature of an otherwise useless phone. For a start, it hardly ever seemed to pick up a signal – even in London. She had no chance out here.

As she turned towards east, she stopped and looked at the viewfinder, then up at the moor.

A man was standing in the distance looking straight at her. She could see a dark silhouette on the horizon, just below the dark clouds. She waved, but got no response. She took the picture anyway; she could always Photoshop him out later.

She headed back to the car and looked again to the shape on the horizon. He, if it had been a he, had disappeared. She felt a shiver go down her spine again. *Jesus, its cold out here.* The wind had picked up in the last few minutes, carrying a faint sound with it, but she couldn't make it out.

She looked at the car, and could hear the bass sounds of Led Zep and see James' head banging in time with the music. She glanced at the gorse bush and grinned to herself.

She crept over to it quietly. Maybe she could give Mark a little welcome to Dartmoor whilst James was distracted. She jumped around the gorse bush, big grin fixed on her face but it fell almost immediately. Mark wasn't there.

He'd disappeared.

Mark walked behind the gorse bush, grumbling to himself. *Fucking car. So much money and it still doesn't work properly.* He undid his belt and pulled the buttons on his jeans apart. Instantly cold wind blew in and he shivered. He started to urinate on the gorse bush, sighing with relief as his bladder emptied. Through the gaps in the branches he could see Elana taking pictures with her phone. In the distance he heard a faint rat-tat-tat but he paid it no attention.

He finally stopped and buttoned himself up again, still watching Elana through the branches. *It would be funny to sneak up on her. It'd be worth being shouted at just to see the look on her face.*

Rat-tat-tat.

Louder now. It was an insistent pattern, like someone banging a drum. Mark turned towards the sound and the ground gave way, making him slip. He noticed then that he was standing on the edge of a deep gully. The long grass and gorse bushes had managed to hide it from him in his rush to relieve himself. His feet continued to slide down to the gully and he stretched out to try and grab hold of something.

His hand closed around the edge of a gorse branch and he swore as the thorns dug into his palm. He let go immediately and the slip turned into an outright fall as he tumbled to the bottom of the gully.

"Damn it!" he said, picking himself up off the ground. Thick mud caked the back of his jeans and jumper, and he shook bits of grass out of his hair. *I'm a Muppet.* The road was at least ten feet above his head, the track of his fall/slide quite clear on the steep side of the bank. *Won't take long to climb back out.*

Rat-tat-tat.

It was louder down here. He looked around to see if he could see the source of the noise. He was at the bottom of the gully and water oozed around his feet. He guessed that he was lucky it hadn't rained in a while; the mud was thick enough as it was and he didn't want to think about water rushing through this gully.

People die on Dartmoor every year.

Rat-tat-tat.

"What is that?" he asked aloud. There were no birds in sight, but there was a solitary tree off to his right. Its gnarled and bare branches testament to how long it had stood there. He took a few steps closer to it and the noise got louder.

Rat-tat-tat.

19

It was very cold in the gully, colder than it had been up top. *Should be warmer, it's more sheltered down here.* He started to shake slightly, trembling muscles trying to warm him. *There can't be a woodpecker banging on the bark at this time of year.* He stopped, wondering just what he was trying to do. The noise was more insistent now as well as louder.

Rat-tat-tat.

He turned back to the bank, feeling the cold bite into him again. There was something mournful about the sound; something quite deliberately sad. He could make the noise out more clearly now: it was the banging of a drum, like in a parade or military band. He shivered.

Better start climbing. Now.

He started to scramble up the bank, but slipped and slid back down into the gully.

"Mark!" She called again. The wind was taking her voice away and even though she knew she was shouting she could barely hear herself.

"Down here!"

The voice was faint, but clear. She looked down and had a brief moment of vertigo as she saw Mark struggling to climb up the side of the bank. He was covered in mud and looked thoroughly annoyed.

No, the look on his face wasn't that; it was something else. She felt relief at seeing him, even though it had been less than two minutes since she'd realised he was gone.

"Careful!" he shouted. "It's slippery on the edge."

She stepped back, but craned her neck forward so that she could still see him.

Mark wasn't looking at her, however. Instead, he was staring into the gully behind him. She called his name again and he looked back at her, wild eyed.

"Can you hear that?" he yelled.

"Hear what?" She couldn't hear anything other than the wind.

Mark looked back into the gully.

Rat-tat-tat.

It was right in his ear. He jumped and looked for the cause of the sound. Something moved in his peripheral vision, but when he tried

20

to focus on it, there was nothing there. He ran up the rest of the bank, fear driving him onwards like a rat up a drain pipe. His feet found purchase despite the thick mud underfoot as his legs powered him up the rest of the slope.

Rat-tat-tat.

Fainter now, but he was sure about the noise he'd heard, but that was insane. He looked back into the gully, but couldn't see anything. There wasn't another soul for miles; a car hadn't gone past them for at least an hour and no walkers were brave enough to face the wind and cold. Above all else, definitely no-one playing the drums.

"Jesus, you're filthy," Elana said.

Mark looked at her with those wild eyes for a second, before seeming to calm down.

"Did you hear that?"

"Hear what?"

"The drumming."

"Drumming?" Elana paused, like she was trying to strain her ears. "No. What happened to you?"

"You can't hear that?"

"Mark, I can't hear anything bar you shouting. Let's go back to the car, its cold out here."

"I fell," Mark said.

"Yeah, and look at the state of you."

He looked back again, looking down at the solitary tree. Underneath the mud, he looked pale and he was trembling slightly. Something had unnerved him.

"Come on," she said, taking his muddy hand. He winced slightly and she realised he was cut. "You okay?"

"Yeah," he smiled at her, but was frowning at the same time. "Just tried to use a gorse bush as a brake. It wasn't a good idea."

"Guess not." She kissed him gently on the cheek. "Let's get to the car – you can change your clothes and we can test out that first aid kit."

They crossed back over the road and headed for the car. James was still head-banging obliviously in the front seat. He looked up as they approached and started laughing. He got out and doubled over, laughing far more hysterically than the situation warranted. The sight of him made Mark smile, then start laughing and eventually Elana joined in.

When the laughter faded, Elana opened the boot and retrieved the first aid kit and clean clothes for Mark. Whilst she was gone, James nudged Mark in the ribs.

"So did she jump you?"

"No." Mark looked pained. "I just fell down a bank and ended up in the mud."

"You twat."

"Yep." Mark examined his hand in the fading light. It wasn't that bad, just a couple of scratches.

Elana returned and opened the first aid kit. She dabbed at his hand with an antiseptic wipe and then continued to wipe his hand clean of the mud.

"I don't suppose you heard anything?" Mark asked James.

"I heard the talents of Messers Page and Plant accompanied by the wonderful Bonham and miserable Jones." James said. "What was I supposed to have heard?"

"Mark heard someone playing the drums," Elana said.

"What out here?" James looked around the moor. The daylight had now faded enough that if there had been any houses, lights would have been burning by now. "Nobody here but us chickens."

"I heard it." Mark pulled his jeans off and winced as cold wind bit into his legs. He quickly tugged on the fresh pair that Elana had got for him.

"You heard someone playing the drums?" James started laughing again. "You've gone mental, mate."

"I'm serious," Mark said, but his voice suggested that he was beginning to doubt himself too. "When I fell, there was this banging, like rat-tat-tat, just like in a, you know, marching band."

"When was the last time you saw a marching band?"

"I was about twelve."

"Well, that's ok then. You heard some banging, thought it was a marching band, and that's not at all mental out here is it?" James shook his head. "We haven't even had a drink yet."

"Well, you had a pint-"

"Yeah, alright Elana, who's counting?" James shook his head again. "Shotgun."

Elana tutted as he climbed back into the car and turned the stereo on again. She watched as he switched the CD out again and threw it into the glove box. Lots of other CDs were out of their cases and he rummaged through the pile. *Well, that's going to annoy Mark. Maybe now he'll finally switch to digital music.*

Mark was staring back across the road again.

"Come on," Elana said, tugging on his sleeve. "Let's get to Tom's house, eh?"

"OK," he said. "This place gives me the creeps."

Mark turned the engine on and scowled as the temperature gauge showed -4 °C with a warning beep.

"No shit," he muttered.

"What's up? Still can't find your cock because it's so small?"

"Can we just go?" Elana demanded. It was nearly dark outside now, the black of night rushing in quicker than the tide. Thick cloud overhead added to the darkness and sense of oppression.

"Yeah." Mark pulled a big U-turn back onto the main road. Another light flashed on the dashboard informing him that the traction control was working. He put his foot down and the car surged forward. *We'll be there in an hour.*

The first flakes of snow began to fall.

Chapter 4

The snow was just the icing on the cake as far as Jeff was concerned. The thick white fog had slowly spread and the first fingers of it were grasping at the rocks they were headed for. *Trust your GPS*. It was still unsettling to see the creep of the fog towards them though. *Like it's doing it on purpose*. He dismissed the thought immediately. *Don't be stupid*.

"Snow," he muttered. "That's just great."

"Don't worry, honey," Sandra called in what he thought of as her bright voice. "It's less than a mile now. We'll be there in fifteen minutes if we're quick."

"What if we get snowed in?"

"Don't be daft. They'd have said on the weather if it was going to be heavy snow. We'll be fine."

"Famous last words."

"I can't believe you're complaining about being snowed in and trapped – in a pub!"

The wind seemed to have picked up in the last couple of minutes and the snow was being driven towards them. Jeff squinted as a flake landed on his eyebrow and he tugged the zip of his jacket upwards despite it being at the top already. Psychologically, it made him feel better.

"Jesus, it's cold. I hope that monk has got into cover."

"Me too," Sandra said, smiling at him. The snow was settling in her hair, making her look whiter than she already was.

The landscape was being transformed before their eyes: snow already lay on the ground and the gorse. The wind was blowing the flakes almost horizontally now whilst also speeding up the progress of the thick mist, which enveloped them moments later, turning the day from grey to white. With the thick snow, the whiteout was almost complete.

"Oh my God," Sandra said and stopped. Jeff almost walked into her.

"Jesus," he said.

"I can't see anything."

They looked at each other, and Jeff was unnerved to see panic in his wife's eyes.

"We've got the GPS, we'll be ok," he said, holding up the grey box with a grin. He looked at the screen and his face fell. Where had once been crystal clear, full colour, sunlight readable display was now a blank screen. "Damn."

"What's wrong?"

"Screen's not working." He banged on the side of the unit and swore again.

"Is it the batteries?"

"Should be good for sixteen hours," he said. "We haven't been out here that long, despite how it feels."

Snow was settling on them as they stood.

"We need to go," Sandra said.

"Yes."

"Follow the path and hope it leads to the pub." She looked at her map. Snowflakes landed on the plastic and she brushed them off. "Even if it doesn't, it'll lead to a road and then we can get a lift or find the pub."

"Good idea," Jeff said. "Let's go."

He strode forward, looking more energised than at any other point that day. In that instant, she loved him again. It was all for her benefit, she realised: he had sensed her worry and was taking charge.

"It's working!" he exclaimed, holding the GPS aloft like it was a trophy at the world cup. He looked at it and for a brief moment the compass showed north behind them and Dartmoor was mapped out around them. "Yes!"

Sandra looked over his shoulder at the device. "Where's Huntleigh?"

"Huntleigh?" He tapped the side of the machine and the picture grew fuzzy, like a film going out of focus. It sharpened again, showing that they were standing on Church Road in a village called Huntleigh. "I've heard of that."

"Yes, but we're not there," Sandra said with as much patience as she could muster.

"No." Snowflakes landed on the screen as it went soft focus again. This time it showed their actual position, surrounded by greenery. A path showed as being slightly off to their right. Jeff looked at his feet, which were planted firmly on a well-established path and scowled at the machine.

The compass needle started spinning, slowly at first then faster and faster. Before either of them could say anything, the entire display went black.

"Useless piece of shit," Jeff said.

"Language," Sandra scolded.

"Sandy, we're stuck in the middle of Dartmoor, with no GPS, it's snowing and I'm really cold. Now is a perfect time to swear."

She didn't say anything, but looked around her, trying to pick out landmarks. It was no use, the whiteout was almost total. A knot of anxiety began to form in her stomach.

"We should follow the path. If we look down, we can see it."

"Good idea," she said. "Let's hope there's not more than one path."

With that comforting thought, they kept walking. Jeff took the lead, striding in the direction that had briefly shown as "South" before the compass had started spinning. Silently he ran through a list of exactly what he would say to the shopkeeper when he returned the GPS on Monday. *Hell, I'll make the trip to Exeter tomorrow especially. Accurate to within three metres my arse.*

Sandra kept the map in her hand, but it was next to useless now. She wished she'd brought a compass, but it had been her idea to test the GPS. She could just make out Jeff's shape ahead of her and called for him to slow down. Everything was so quiet, the snow seemed to act as a sound dampener. She called again and nearly walked into him, he stopped so quickly.

"We're going downhill."

"That's good," she said. "From what I remember, we go downhill for about quarter of a mile, then the pub is on our right."

"Maybe this fog will clear as we go down."

He was wrong. Visibility stayed at a couple of feet as they carefully made their way down the track. It had widened out as they'd gone over the top and they were now walking side by side. A dark shape loomed ahead of them.

Sandra grabbed his arm hard enough to hurt.

"Relax, it's a cairn," he said. The mist cleared around the mound of stones. It was nearly as high as him and clearly very old.

"It's called King's Oven," Sandra said. "Something to do with King Arthur, I think."

Jeff gave her a pained look. "Can we save the history lesson for when we're somewhere warmer?"

"Of course, sorry hon."

Snow was now nearly ankle deep around the edges of the path and the ground they could see was rapidly turning white. Their footsteps were disappearing as they walked. Jeff had never seen snow like it.

"This snow is crazy."

"Yes," Sandra said. "But we're really close now."

"You've been saying that for ages."

"The Cairn is just up the hill from the pub." She smiled, although they could barely see each other. "We're going to be warm in less than fifteen minutes."

"Great," he said without enthusiasm. He resisted pointing out that there was no way they were leaving the pub in this weather; in fact they would probably have to stay for the night unless the snow stopped in the next half an hour. As the thought crossed his mind, the wind picked up again and the snow fell as fast and heavy as rain.

No, not going anywhere tonight.

Before he really registered any change underfoot, he suddenly realised that he was standing on tarmac. The snow was getting deep, but his feet sank through it to hit the firmer surface underneath.

"A road!" His excitement verged on the ridiculous.

"This way!" Sandra said, turning right and almost running down the road.

"How do you know?"

"Trust me!"

That's what got us into this mess. She had disappeared into the fog, so he did a cross between a jog and walk that ended up being slower than both. A sign slowly came into view. The name of the pub was obscured by a large banner proclaiming that the pub had a new owner.

"Shit, I hope it's open," Jeff muttered.

"Language!" Sandra stepped out of the mist. She kissed him on the cheek, brushing cold lips against his colder cheek. "It is open. Come on, I'll get you a pint."

"Fantastic."

"Yes, we might as well get comfortable. I don't think we're going anywhere for a while."

Chapter 5

Within minutes it was snowing hard enough for the wipers to be on full speed. Mark flicked the heaters on, pressing a button until the display in front of him said 20 °C, then switched the heated windscreen on. His headlights only served to illuminate how heavily it was snowing.

"Jesus," James said.

Mark nodded in agreement. "That's pretty mad snow."

"We're relatively high up at the moment," Elana said, examining the map. Her finger traced the contour lines. "We'll be in Princetown soon, maybe we can stop somewhere till this blows over."

Mark and James exchanged a look. "Nah, let's push on," Mark said. "Pasty's expecting us, and we're nearly there now.

"It's at least another thirty miles from here," Elana said. She was using her thumb to estimate the distance. *It could be a lot more.* She didn't voice the thought.

Princetown flashed by quickly, basically some houses and a roundabout. It was still snowing heavily: huge white flakes pelted the windscreen, and it had already settled on the roof tops and the verge. They were yet to see another car and no people walked the streets.

"Do you think the locals know something we don't?" James muttered.

"We could try listening to the radio," Elana said.

Mark flicked a switch on the steering wheel and got static for his troubles. He flicked again and the radio displayed 'searching'. The word blinked on and off on the display for several minutes then he gave up and switched the CD back on.

"No radio," he said.

"That's crazy," Elana said.

"We're in the middle of nowhere," James said. "This is Devon - they probably still have tube fired radios and TVs down here."

"Don't be an idiot," Elana said. "Lots of places down here have fibre optic broadband. It's probably as fast here as it is at home."

"And, pray tell, how do you know that?"

"She wants to move here," Mark explained. "She can make a persuasive argument."

"What, by talking about broadband speeds? Jesus, Mark!"

"Take a look out of the window. That's why."

James turned his head to look out the passenger window. Darkness spread out before him obscuring everything more than ten metres away. Thick snowflakes continued to fall heavily, melting into large drops of water as soon as they touched the glass, converging to form small rivers on the window.

"Looks fantastic," James said.

"It is," Elana said, with no trace of irony.

"Look in the daylight," Mark said. "It's beautiful down here."

"You're serious aren't you?" James said, looking at his old friend. "You'll come and live here, leave the city behind?"

Mark nodded. "It has a huge appeal."

"What about work?"

"I can do three days in the office, rest of the time work from home. Good broadband you see," Mark said, with a smile. "I've already talked to my boss about this."

"What!?" James roared. "You talked to your boss before me?"

"Oh, grow up," Elana said.

"Keep out of this, I'm talking to my friend."

"Don't speak to her like that," Mark said, his brow creasing in annoyance.

James sank back into his chair, crossing his arms with a huff, like a child. "You've only been together what, less than a year?"

"Eighteen months," Mark and Elana said at the same time.

"So you're giving everything up for some bint you've only been with for just over a year?"

"Hey, I can hear you, you-" Elana started.

"Give it a rest James," Mark interrupted. *Great, my best friend and girlfriend arguing. This is going to be a brilliant weekend.* "We're moving to the country, not Mars."

"Same fucking thing,"

"You are such a child," Elana muttered.

30

Silence descended on them thicker than the snow outside. The CD had finished and so all they could hear was the soft whirring of the windscreen wipers as they fought to keep the view clear.

"This is pretty bad," Mark said eventually.

"We'll be ok," James said.

Elana watched the road go by. The snow was definitely settling now, small mounds lining the side of the road. None was sticking to the road ahead, though. Not yet.

"Where are we anyway?" she asked.

Mark switched the SatNav back on and waited for it to calibrate and find them. "We're on the B3212, heading east, ish."

Elana flicked her passenger light on and looked at the map. "So we're heading for Moretonhampstead, right?"

Mark shrugged. "That's what the SatNav says, but there's no guarantee of that now is there?"

"It seems to be working now," James said. He seemed to have calmed down slightly, but Mark knew that the anger would still be simmering away underneath. James never forgave anything easily.

"It's still nearly thirty miles to Pasty's house," Elana said, using her thumb on the map again.

"You said that half an hour ago," James complained.

"We're not going very fast," Mark said, gesturing at the speedometer. It had not risen above twenty since it had started snowing.

"Put your foot down then," James said.

"Not in this."

"You wuss. Worried about scratching your new car? Pathetic."

"No," Mark said as calmly as he could. "Worried about crashing. There could be ice out there."

"Oh for God's sake, it's only been below freezing for the last hour or so. There won't be black ice in that time will there?"

"Hey, you can walk if you want to," Elana said.

James didn't reply. He stared out the front windscreen watching the hypnotic steady fall of the snow. "I need a beer."

Thick white fog rolled around them and obscured everything from view.

"Well that's just great," Mark said. The headlights seemed to bounce straight back off the fog. Visibility had gone down to no further than the end of the bonnet. He could still see the thick snowflakes but only when they crossed directly in front of the headlights. The fog was denser than any he'd ever seen. He eased back off the accelerator and their already tawdry speed fell further. The needle hovered between zero and ten.

"Use the SatNav," James said.

"This isn't Colin McRae," Mark said.

"Easy right," James said. "Maybe."

"Slow down," Elana said.

"If I go any slower we stop."

"Maybe we should." The view out of Elana's window had become absolutely obscured. She shivered. "Turn the heating up, please hon."

Mark turned the heating to its highest setting and was greeted by a blast of warm air. The air-con showed twenty five degrees, but it felt colder. The white outside seemed to seep into the car.

The gorse bushes that lined the road became dark shadows of mythical proportions. What had once been skinny branches topped with thorns became thick tentacles reaching out to ensnare the car. The thorns made the bushes look like snarling animals through the mist. Elana shivered.

A large shape ran onto the road ahead of them.

Mark swore and slammed his feet on the brakes. The back of the car snaked out on the rapidly settling snow and they started to slide slowly towards the dark shape. Elana held her hands over her face when her door hit the shape. She heard the thump of the door crumpling, but the glass didn't break. The car stopped sliding with the impact.

"What the fuck was that?" James shrieked.

Elana's heart thumped loudly in her ears. Her knuckles were white where she was gripping the seat. The mist and snow obscured the view out the window and she opened the door slowly.

"Jesus," Mark said, "my new car!"

"What the fuck was that?" James' voice was still high pitched. "Seriously, I'm not fucking about, what was that?"

Elana felt the bite of the wind and the mist seemed to seep into the car. Snow landed on her hair as she leant out of the doorway.

"Els, what you doing hun?"

"I'm going to see what we hit."

"You'll freeze out there."

"What if we hit a person? They could die." With that, she stepped into the cold. Snow made her hair white instantly. The mist swirled around her. Now she was in it, it didn't seem as thick as when they were moving. She could see the edge of the road and the gorse bushes there. Looking back at the car, she could see her door had a large dent in it, but no metal was exposed; it would be easily fixed. She headed for the back of the car, guessing correctly that the thing would be behind them following the slide. She took one look at it then ran back to the car.

"It's a sheep," she said.

"You're fucking kidding!" James said in something close to his normal voice. "That thing was huge."

"Just the mist messing with you," she said.

"Is it-" Mark started.

"Yeah, it's dead. We need to move it off the road."

"I'm not going out there," James said.

"We have to," Mark said.

Elana nodded agreement. "If something else comes along in this and hits it, they won't just have some mutton to take home."

Grumbling, James opened his door shortly after Mark opened his and they jogged back to the sheep. They awkwardly picked it up by its legs and shuffled to the nearest verge. Once there, they could only see the rear fog lights of the Audi to guide their way back.

"This fog is mental," Mark said when they returned to the car.

"I thought it wasn't so bad when you were walking in it," Elana said.

"You're crazy," James said. "I couldn't see the end of my nose."

Mark agreed with him. "We need to get off the road. We might not be so lucky with the next thing we meet." He turned the engine on and eased the car forward. They were moving even more slowly now.

"We just killed a sheep," Elana said. Mark hadn't said anything about the dent in the car door, which told her that he must be concerned more about the mist.

"Only got in before the farmer," James said. "We should chuck it in the boot and sell it to some yokels."

"Yokels?" Elana exclaimed.

"You'd have to explain that we killed it in the first place. That might not go down well," Mark said.

"Easy money," James said.

"And how much does one sheep fetch on the open market today?"

"Don't give me your banker shite now, Mark," James said. "It was just an idea."

"A stupid one."

They drove on in silence following that exchange. The mist didn't ease; it didn't get worse either. It was just there, an omnipresent white wall obscuring the beautiful landscape they were travelling through. Every now and then, a large snow flake was visible through the fog. Elana imagined the whole world turning white, hidden behind the white mist.

"I don't like this," Mark said, eventually.

"What?" James asked. He hadn't turned the stereo back on, the tension in the car was getting to him too.

"I can't see anything. We need to stop."

"We can't stop here." James gestured out the window. "This is a back road somewhere on the way to the middle of nowhere."

"He's right," Elana surprised herself by saying. "We can't stop here."

"We need to get out of this fog. We need to stop and let it clear," Mark said.

"If we stop here, how long will the car stay warm?" Elana asked.

"No idea," he said. "Couple of hours maybe. We could keep the engine running."

"And run out of fuel, so when the fog clears we can't go anywhere?" Elana said.

"You're a fucking idiot," James said, looking at his friend.

"I'll be a 'fucking idiot' to keep driving in this," Mark punctuated the phrase by making the inverted commas with his fingers, keeping the palms of his hands on the steering wheel as he did so.

"We can't stop," Elana said. "We'll freeze out here."

"We could come off the road if we keep going," Mark pointed out. "Then we'd be really in trouble."

"It's still snowing," she said. "If it snows all night, we could end up buried. No-one would find us and then we'd die out here."

"I'm not dying in fucking Devon," James said.

"Relax," Mark said, "no-one's going to die. We'll just pull over until the fog clears then we'll be on our way. Phone Pasty, tell him where we are."

Elana pulled her phone out at the same time as James. "No signal," they said simultaneously.

"Of course not," Mark muttered. The car was still easing forward, less than ten miles an hour. The clock on the dashboard showed 6:06 pm. "It's not that late, we can style this out."

"Seriously, Mark, we can't," Elana said, the strain cracking her voice. She had to make him understand: no-one would find them up here. This time of year, there might not be any traffic on this road for several days.

"As much as I hate to say it, but I reckon she's right," James said. "Look, let's see if we can find a house or something ok?"

Mark nodded assent and they rolled forward again. Without warning, the headlights picked out a large white sign. The bottom half seemed to swim into view through the mist. It promised real ales, cream teas and accommodation. The top half was obscured by an "under new management" banner.

"Yes!" Mark exclaimed, relief flooding through him. He pulled into the verge next to a large building that was still mostly obscured by the fog.

"What a result," James said. "We've found a fucking pub!"

Part Two: The Early Hours

"There's a corpse in the ottoman at the foot of my bed."

Chapter 6

Jeff sank half a pint in one big, satisfied gulp. He had been hugely relieved to see that they served Otter Ale. Sandra had asked for vodka, lime and soda and they sat on two rickety old bar stools, relishing the warmth.

"It's snowing then," the barman said. He was younger than Jeff by about ten years, making him still the right side of forty. His clothes sat easily on him, creating a smart look, even though he was only wearing jeans and a shirt. From the way Sandra was looking at him, he was good looking too.

"Yes," Jeff said, taking a smaller sip this time. "Really foggy too."

"Yeah, we were warned about that."

"Warned?" Sandra asked. "There was no mention of it on the weather before we set out."

"Sorry, no, that's not what I meant." The barman smiled. "I'm Bruce Singer, this is my pub." Jeff shook hands with him, but wasn't entirely sure why. Sandra told him their names. "Me and the wife have only been open here a couple of weeks. The locals told us the weather could change quickly."

"Uz did." This came from the only other person in the pub. His Devonian accent was so thick, it took Jeff a few seconds to realise what had just been said. He turned to see a thickset man with the skin of an outdoors worker.

Bruce coloured at the comment. He smiled at Sandra, but it was a weary smile, before turning back to the man. "Anyhow. Adam, isn't it about time you were heading home?"

"I'll go dreckly." His accent made it sound like he missed all the vowels from the word. "Give uz another fer thikky road." He waved his empty glass at Bruce.

Bruce rolled his eyes at Jeff and Sandra then refilled the glass. He put it down in front of Adam, who muttered, "Proper job."

"So you live round here?" Bruce asked. He directed the question at Jeff, but was looking at Sandra.

"We live near Torrington," Jeff said.

"Wow, that's a long way away," Bruce said.

"We thought we'd do more walking, see the countryside around our house," Sandra said.

"Tid'n near your house missus," Adam said, but was ignored by everybody.

"How far have you walked today?"

"Too bloody far."

"About ten miles," Sandra spoke over Jeff. "We came over the Moor. It was beautiful until the fog came. We thought we could get a bus back to our car."

Bruce looked at his watch and shook his head. "Won't be another bus today. Last one goes just after four in the winter."

"Brilliant," Jeff said. "So now we're stuck here."

"What about a taxi? We'll just do that instead."

Bruce smiled. "When it stops snowing, I can get you a taxi number. Till then, do you want a look at the menu?"

Sandra took a menu and started reading it. Jeff looked around the bar, taking it in for the first time. The main bar room was rectangular, but looked more interesting due to the wooden beams that ran along its low ceiling. The walls were a traditional white, with black struts at regular intervals from ceiling to floor. *Regular, but not even. This place is old.*

The bar itself sat in a corner on the right hand side of the room. Whiskey bottles lined the shelves behind the actual bar, and Jeff counted four different bottles of vodka. Several bottles of liqueur rounded of an impressive collection of alcohol. Next to the shelves, two real ale barrels sat on stands, tipped forward slightly ready to serve. His gaze drifted left of the bar and he spied a doorway marked "Private, Guests Only." Adjacent to this, a small corridor led into a dark alcove. Jeff peered into it and he could just make out a dartboard on the far wall. *Not a corridor at all, but an oche.* For some reason, this made Jeff smile. Behind him, enough tables to sit five different groups lay scattered around the floor space.

On the same wall as the door to the restaurant, a large fireplace occupied the remaining space. The fire was burning well, flames jumping high on the logs. Jeff slid off his stool and stood in front of the fire, letting the warmth spread throughout his body. A small plaque sat in the middle of the crossbeam and he bent to read it.

"Burning since September 1845"

He smiled to himself. *The things these old pubs do to get tourists in.* He rubbed his hands and held them out to the fire. They had both stripped off their waterproof coats and trousers when they had walked in, and he considered moving his things to in front of the fire to dry them. Instead he went back to the bar and drank more of his pint.

"The rabbit pie sounds nice," Sandra said, showing him the menu.

"Have it then. I'll have the beef and ale."

"Don't you want to look at the menu? Maybe have something different?"

"No, places like this always have beef and ale pie and that'll do me."

"We do a fantastic pie," Bruce said, pulling a notepad from his pocket.

Jeff smiled and nodded. "With chips please."

Sandra ordered the rabbit pie, with new potatoes and another vodka. Jeff sighed to himself. *Tears by eight o'clock.*

"That's a lovely fire," he said.

"Yes, it's nice and warm in here," Sandra said.

"It's been burning since 1845," added Jeff.

"I know," Sandra said and turned to look at the fire. "I've been here before remember?"

"Just saying that's what the plaque says."

"Yes it has," Bruce said. "It's quite famous round here." He started to wipe a few glasses as he talked. "The pub was originally on the other side of the road, but it burned down. They built this one, then carried the ashes over from the old building. They were still smouldering so they built a fire and it's burned ever since, apparently." He smiled. "Good story, huh?"

Jeff snorted into his pint. "Load of crap."

"Jeff," Sandra warned.

"Ah, come on. A fire that's burned every day for over a hundred and fifty years?" It'll have been pretty hot on some of those days. It's just a story to give the place something different so tourists will come."

"You may be right Jeff, but there is more to the tale," Bruce said.

"Ee be right," Adam said. "'Fire eve bin gwain every day since I bin yer."

"Yeah, and how long's that?"

"All me life." Adam looked Jeff in the eye. "This yer be Dartmoor, some things be best left as they be 'n not talked about." He waved his hand at the fire.

"What's he talking about?" Jeff asked Bruce, trying to suppress a laugh. *What a bumpkin. Quick, get a phone, The Wurzels are missing a member.*

"Story goes that the Devil used to frequent this place till it burned down. Since then, the fire has been lit to keep him away," Bruce said.

"The Devil?" Jeff said, this time the laugh escaping his lips. "Jesus Christ."

"Dawnt joke about what 'ee dawnt understand." Adam warned.

"Ah, come on!"

Adam's face remained stern. Jeff scowled and returned his gaze to his pint. No point arguing with locals, the man was clearly a fool. Adam was not to be dissuaded however.

"You knaw nort," he snarled. "This yer place be older then uz knaw, volk eve lived yer on Dartmoor fer thousands of yers – thikky things can't be explained"

"You're talking out your arse," Jeff said without thinking.

Adam leapt off his stool and pushed past Sandra to grab Jeff by the throat. He squeezed slightly and Jeff started to choke.

"I zeed things with me own eyes," Adam said, his voice surprisingly calm. "You think I'm some kind of mump aid but you'll zee. Stay ere on Dartmoor long enough and you'll zee."

Jeff started to see black in the periphery of his vision. Stars swam into view as he heard Sandra shouting. He felt a faint thump, thump as she hit Adam's arm, but there was no give in the grip. Bruce was shouting something, but it was no use.

The world was going black.

Chapter 7

"We interrupting something?" James said loudly. He grinned at the room as Mark and Elana came in behind him, bundled up against the cold. Mark frowned at the scene before him. A burly, rugged looking man held an older man by the throat whilst a woman battered at his arm and the barman yelled at them all.

"My kind of pub," James said in a stage whisper to Mark.

The burly man let the other go with snarl. He stared at the newcomers with undisguised disdain whilst the older man sagged to the floor coughing. The barman rushed to his side, supporting his head and looking at him with genuine concern.

"We should leave," Elana said.

"We can't," Mark said, with a better whisper than James had managed. "The weather's too bad."

"Adam, get out of my pub!" the barman yelled. "You're barred!"

"This place doesn't look very nice," Elana said.

"It's warm," Mark nodded at the fire. "Let's at least warm up for a bit, let the weather break."

"Tid'n your pub, buye, dawnt worry Bruce, I baint comin' back yer," Adam said, glaring at everyone in the room. He stomped back to his stool and picked up a coat.

"Jesus, I can't get that banging out of my head," Mark said to Elana, shaking his head.

"You're thinking of that now?"

"Banging?" Adam said, suddenly standing next to them.

"Hey, back off," James said, stepping forward and putting his hand on Adam's chest.

Adam looked James up and down with utter contempt. "Bangin' like thikky drum?"

43

Mark looked at Adam with his mouth open. "Yeah, exactly like that. Rat-tat-tat. It's driving me mad."

"Mark, don't speak to the local psycho ok?" James said. His hand was still on Adam's chest. "How the fuck can you understand him anyway?"

Adam stepped back and slipped his coat off. He shook his head. "Maybe there's time."

"You're not welcome here, Adam." Bruce roared. "You need to leave, now!"

Adam glared at Bruce, but shook his head once more. He turned his coat inside out and slipped it back on. The woolly fleece lining had seen better days, with bobbles marring the surface like acne on a teenager. He opened the door to the pub, pausing as cold wind blasted in, carrying a few flakes of snow, and then left without another word.

"I'm so sorry," Bruce said to the man who was still coughing. "Would you like another drink, Jeff? It's on the house."

"Got... to... drive... later," Jeff said between coughs.

"I don't think you'll be driving anywhere anytime soon, mate, it's chucking it down with snow outside," James said.

"He's right," Mark said from his place by the fire. "It's really foggy and snowing hard. We had to stop."

"Can I get you a drink?" Bruce asked.

"Yes," James said, pulling out his wallet. He turned to Mark and Elana. "What do you want guys?"

"Beer for me, whatever you're having will do, and a white wine for Els," Mark said. He rubbed his hands and held them to the fire. His brow was creased, thick lines marring his good looks.

"Want one yourself, mate?" *The last time Mark looked like that, we were doing our finals.*

"No thanks," Bruce said. "I've a pub to run." He smiled at James and took his money.

"How bad is the snow now?" Jeff asked.

"As I said, you can't see anything." James answered. "Don't think any of us are going anywhere tonight unless it stops in the next half hour or so."

"That's just great."

"What about that horrible man who left?" Sandra asked.

"Don't worry about him," Bruce said. "He lives in the cottage about half a mile back down the road. He'll be home by now."

44

"What are you worrying about him for?" Jeff asked with more anger than he'd intended. "He tried to kill me."

"Don't be so melodramatic, darling." Sandra rolled her eyes at James. Jeff saw the look and the anger intensified for a second. *Psycho nearly kills me and she's making eyes at the new pretty boy.*

"The snow is nothing to worry about," Bruce smiled and raised his voice so everyone could hear him. "We've got rooms upstairs and you can all stay tonight. The roads should be clear by the morning."

"Best have a pint then," James said nodding at Jeff. "What's your poison mate?"

"My name is Jeff and I hate that expression – it's very American." Jeff paused for a second. "And don't call me mate."

"He's very tired," Sandra said.

"No worries," James said. "I was just trying to be friendly." He scooped up the three drinks and crossed back to Mark and Elana. "Did you hear that?"

"Yes," Elana said. "This is a small pub and we're not deaf."

"And they can hear whatever you're about to say," Mark said, picking up his pint "Cheers."

"I wasn't going to say anything."

"Yes you were," Elana said. "Thanks for the drink."

"You ok, buddy? You look awful."

"I keep hearing that rat-tat-tat." Mark said. "I can't get it out of my head."

"Ah come on," James said. "It was the wind howling through the trees or a bird or something."

"It's January," Elana said.

"We have birds in January," James said. "Some of us have birds all year round."

"That supposed to be funny?"

"No, it *was*," James said with a grin.

"You're a child."

"Guys, cut it out, ok?" Mark said. "What are we going to do? It looks like we're stuck here for the night."

"We could get utterly shit faced," James suggested.

"I was thinking more about ringing Pasty and telling him we won't be there tonight," Mark said.

"That too."

Jeff rubbed his neck, wincing. He could still feel the large hands pinching into his windpipe, cutting off his air. He knew without looking that red finger marks blotched his skin. Frustration boiled within him; all his life he had been walked on, made to feel a fool. Now this: physically intimidated by an idiot who seemed to believe in the devil and all that nonsense. *Unbelievable.*

Sandra was still sitting next to him, though she kept throwing furtive glances at the newcomers. *She thinks I'm blind.* He drank long from his pint to disguise the bitterness. *Hide bitter with bitter. Somebody, somewhere, would find that funny.*

The door to the side of the bar marked 'private' swung open and a young woman walked through carrying two precariously balanced plates. From the way she carried them, it was clear that she had not been working in a kitchen long.

She had black hair tied back in a bun that made her look severe. Her skin had a slick sheen on it that made her look radiant to Jeff; it was only later that he realised it was sweat. Her kitchen whites were stained in several places, and one of the stains looked a lot like blood. *At least the meat is fresh.*

"Rabbit pie?" she asked. Sandra put her hand straight up like a child in a primary school class. Twenty years ago that had made him chuckle.

The woman put an enormous plate of food in front of Sandra. She turned to Jeff, blue eyes sparkling. "I suppose that means you have the unexciting but inexplicably popular beef and ale pie." She put the other, equally large, plate in front of him. Steam rose from both pies, the pastry crust doing a bad job of containing the juices in the pie dish. "Can I get you anything else?"

"Don't you dare ask for ketchup." Sandra said quietly. More loudly: "Just some salt please."

"No problem."

Bruce smiled at the woman. "Saran, this is Jeff and Sandra. I think they'll be staying the night."

"Staying, but-"

"The weather is awful, dear, it's snowing badly." He smiled again. "They walked here, hoping to get a bus back to their car."

"No buses now it's dark," Saran said. She was easily ten years younger than Jeff.

"We know that now," Jeff said, trying to ease a natural smile onto his face.

"I'll make up one of the rooms." She gestured with her head at the group by the fire. "What about them?"

"I think they'll have to stay, but I'm not sure," Bruce said. "I'll check."

Saran swished her way back through the private door and Jeff turned his attention to the beef pie. Just for a moment then, he had felt almost happy.

"Hi, I'm Bruce." He pulled a chair across from the next table and sat between James and Elana. "You guys ok?"

"Yes, thanks," Mark said.

"What was going on just then?" James asked.

"Just a small disagreement. Adam can be a bit highly strung."

"Just a *small* disagreement? It looked like he was trying to kill him," Elana said.

"Ignoring my friend's trouble with pronouns there for a second, what's it like here on a Saturday night?" James was grinning and nudged Mark with his elbow.

"I'm sure it looked worse than it was," Bruce said. "You guys on holiday?"

"We're on our way to a friend's for the weekend. It's not that far from here actually," Mark said.

"Yeah? Where?"

"Huntleigh."

"I've heard of it," Bruce said. "Why have I heard of it?"

"There was some trouble there last year," Mark said.

For the first time in hours, James looked interested in what somebody else had to say. "You didn't mention this before."

"No point," Mark said with a shrug. "It was nearly six months ago."

"What happened?" James asked.

"Some wolves attacked a couple of the locals. A few people died," Mark said. Elana was scowling at him.

"I remember that!" Bruce said. "That was all happening just as we started to look for a pub to buy. Put us right off the area that did. No offense to your mate, obviously."

"He'd been living there for a couple of years by the time it happened. Vaguely knew one of the guys who died apparently," Mark said. "It's all over now though, and the people there just don't talk about it. Lots of houses for sale there as a result." He smiled at Elana.

"I'm not surprised," Bruce said.

"You could've told me," James said, crossing his arms.

"It didn't occur to me. It's not important."

"Huntleigh is a lovely place. You'd never guess what had happened there," Elana said. "Just forget about it James."

"So," Bruce said after a pause. "It looks like the snow is here to stay. We have three rooms upstairs that you are welcome to use. We're in the process of doing them up so that we can do B&B, but they're not ready yet. They have beds and shower rooms. No charge obviously."

"Really?" James said.

"Yes."

"No, we can't stay for free, we'll give you some money," Elana said.

"Are you mental?"

"Yeah, we'll pay you something."

James swore softly to himself. "The man said no charge. You two are nuts."

"Ignore him Bruce," Mark said. "I don't think we've got a choice about staying at the moment, but can we check the weather later?"

"Of course, of course," Bruce said. "What about something to eat? I'll get you some menus."

He returned moments later with three menus just as the fire sputtered. Bruce put the menus down and crossed to the fire-place. He looked in the log basket and was surprised to see it empty. The fire was down to embers already, although they were still glowing bright red.

"Best get more wood, mate, or that fire's going out for the first time in nearly two hundred years," James said.

"And then the devil will appear. Woo-woo," Jeff said quietly.

Bruce laughed, but it sounded forced. "I'll just go to the wood store. I won't be long, then I'll take your order."

He picked up the log basket and went out the back of the bar. Saran looked at him with eyebrows raised.

"Need more logs," he said and she returned to reading her book. "Those new people need some food." The kitchen was still warm and smelled very strongly of cooked rabbit. His stomach rumbled as he opened the back door to the yard. Two generators hummed next to the oil tank. They provided electricity for the pub and kitchen. Heat came solely from the fire in the pub, with venting taking the warmth around the rooms.

He passed the generators, feeling the hum as a bass note in his chest and opened the door to the log store. He fumbled for the light, the cold suddenly reminding him that he was only wearing a shirt. Snow had already settled enough for his footprints to show the way back to the open kitchen door. The fluorescent light flicked on and Bruce's mouth opened in surprise.

The wood store was completely empty, except for small bits of bark and twigs. The delivery guy was supposed to have come that afternoon, but he hadn't made it judging by the emptiness of the store. Even so, there should have been a couple of bags left in there, so where were they? Bruce looked up at the sky, frowning at the thick flakes falling around him.

It was going to be a cold night.

Chapter 8

"Can I get you guys something to eat?"

James looked up from his pint and smiled. Standing in front of him was a slim woman in her early thirties. He could see a firm figure hidden behind kitchen whites and her skin almost radiated warmth and health. Her black hair was tied in a functional bun and just for a moment he envisaged it falling to her shoulder as she smiled at him. He felt his breath catch in his throat.

"I'm Saran. Bruce seems to have forgotten to ask you what you want to eat."

"Whatever's good," James said, with his best smile. He hadn't needed more than that for years.

"It's all good. I'm the cook."

Mark suppressed a laugh. "I'll have some chips please."

"You don't want more than that?" Elana asked.

"Nah, I'm good. You have more if you want."

She ordered a veggie burger, chips and salad whilst James went for a rabbit pie.

"Can we see the room?" Elana asked, when they were done ordering.

"Sure. None of the rooms are finished yet, though, so make sure you don't tell your friends this is a dump."

Elana laughed. "We're staying for free because of the weather. You could have axe murderers up there and we would still recommend you to our friends."

Saran smiled at her. "I'll get you a key. Have you got any luggage or bags?"

"In the car," Elana said and she stood up. "I'll go and get it."

"No problem." Saran left, with James watching her stroll back across the bar to the kitchen door. It swung shut behind her, the 'Private' sign vibrating with the slam of the door.

"Good lord," James said.

Mark rolled his eyes. "I'll get the bags hon."

"No, it's fine, I'll go."

"Come on, it's freezing out there," Mark said. "Let me go." He turned to James. "Want your bag?"

Elana shrugged, sitting back down whilst James shook his head. Mark drained some of his pint then crossed to the door. He opened it and shivered as the cold wind blew in against him.

"Don't you want your coat?" Elana called.

"Nah, I'll only be thirty seconds." He stepped into the cold, instantly regretting his false machismo. *Man up Mark, it's not that cold.*

But it was. The snow was already over the tops of his shoes and the mist seemed to be freezing in front of him. It was totally silent outside; nothing moved anywhere. The heavy cloak of silence served to unnerve him. *What of all the animals? The sheep, cows, horses. Will they all die tonight?* He shivered, hugging himself. *I've been out here less than five seconds and already my hands and feet are going numb.*

He trudged towards the car, feet sinking in the already thick snow. It was less than ten metres away, but it felt further. Snow had covered the bonnet and roof, making it look like the car had been there for days, not just under an hour. He dug in his pockets and pulled out the remote key, pressing the unlock button. His hazard lights flashed briefly and the car beeped, the sound amplified by the complete deadness around him. He jumped slightly on hearing it.

The boot opened as he approached and he grabbed Elana's small weekend bag. It was light, which was one of the reasons he loved her so much. She didn't go in for the stereotypical girly things: no mammoth shoe shopping sprees; no cupboards full of handbags; no mountain of half used makeup and no perfume bottles half-filled with liquid.

He smiled to himself as he lifted the bag out and slammed the boot shut. He left the other two bags alone. James could come get his if he wanted it and Mark was quite happy to 'scum up' for the night if necessary.

The cold wind blew hard and straight through his shirt, making him shiver. Something made him look over the road, something in the corner of his eye that didn't look right. He stopped, squinting through the snow.

A large dark shape stood shrouded in mist on the other side of the road. Mark felt his breath catch in his throat. The wind blew again and the mist cleared for a moment. Just for a second he had full view of the shape.

It was a man dressed in a full length monk's habit. The brief glimpse didn't allow Mark to see his shoes, but if pressed he would have said that the man was bare foot. His face was completely in shadow, hidden from plain view. The angle of the hood had suggested that the man/monk wasn't looking at Mark.

What was he looking at?

The pub. He's looking at the pub.

"Hey!" Mark shouted. "You ok?"

The mist enveloped them both again. The monk disappeared behind a wall of fog.

"The pub's open!" Mark called, quieter this time and he wouldn't have been able to explain why. "It's warm in there!"

The silence roared on. Mark stepped into the road, heading for where he'd seen the monk, but then he stopped. He started to tremble, muscles convulsing to keep him warm. *I could freeze out here. I might never find him in this mist. I'll walk around for hours, looking for a mad monk. In the morning they'll find my corpse frozen in the snow.*

The last thought made him move with more purpose. He turned back towards the pub and forced himself to jog to the door. The snow was deep enough to make the jog difficult. When he reached the door, and the comfort of the outside light, he turned back to where he'd seen the monk.

The mist swirled and swirled, thick snow adding to the whiteout. Nothing seemed to move bar the snow. Momentarily the mist cleared and he had full view of the other side of the road.

There was nothing there.

No man, no monk.

Did I imagine it? Mark shivered again, although this time not because of the cold. He opened the door and stepped into the warmth of the pub with one thought ringing clearly in his mind.

He had not imagined the monk.

James looked up at the cold blast of air and grinned. Snow had settled on Mark's hair whilst he had been outside and he looked like he'd aged thirty years in the couple of minutes he'd been gone. James' smile faded when he saw the expression on Mark's face.

"What's up?" James said. "You look like you've seen a ghost."

Mark turned sharply, looked like he was going to say something but then clearly thought better of it. He sat down heavily next to Elana and drank the remains of his pint in one go. James noticed that his arm trembled as he lifted the pint. His other hand rested on Elana's leg.

"Get off!" she said. "You're freezing!"

"Sorry," Mark mumbled, putting his empty glass down heavily enough to draw interest from the bar.

"Go stand by the fire," she said. "That'll warm you up."

"What's wrong, mate?" The concern in James' voice sounded unnatural. Elana was surprised.

"There was someone out there."

"What?"

Suddenly everyone in the bar was listening to Mark. Jeff stood up and stood halfway between them and the bar.

"There was someone outside."

"Are they ok?" Jeff asked.

"They'll freeze!" Sandra said.

Mark held up his hands. "Hang on, it was weird."

"Weird how?"

"Let him talk James, for God's sake," Elana said.

"I got your bag," he nodded at Elana, "then noticed this man standing there. Well, at least I think it was a man."

"He's going to freeze! Let's get him in!" Sandra said, joining her husband's side.

Mark shook his head. "He's gone. I went to look for him, but I couldn't find him. I shouted out. It's the fog-" He stopped and shivered. "Maybe I imagined it."

"Great," James said. "Now you're seeing things as well as hearing them."

"What did he look like?" Jeff had a strange expression on his face. Mark met his eyes, an unspoken question in his gaze.

"He was," he paused, "well, he looked like a monk."

"Oh my God, we saw a monk!" Sandra said. "Up on the moor. Maybe it's him, maybe he's lost."

"It's not the same person," Jeff said.

"Why not? How many monks are there in the area?" Sandra demanded.

"It can't be," Jeff said. "He walked the other way."

"We don't know where he walked."

"You saw a monk?" Elana asked.

"Well done, Sherlock," James said, earning himself a pained expression from both Elana and Mark.

"There aren't any monasteries around here," Jeff said. "It's probably that Adam guy messing with us."

"It's freezing out there," Mark said. "Really, really cold. I mean, like, you'll die, it's that cold. I've never seen snow and fog like that in Britain, well anywhere really." He was thinking of skiing in the Alps. *Now, that was cold, but it didn't feel like this.*

"So?"

"Well, it's not the weather for a practical joke is it? No matter how pissed off you are."

Sandra flinched slightly, but Jeff just nodded.

"So what was he doing?"

"I don't know, just standing there, I guess. He was watching the pub."

"I saw a monk!" Elana said. "When we stopped, I saw someone on the moor. It was a monk, I'm sure of it."

"Oh for fuck's sake." James stood up and went to the bar. "If we're talking about disappearing clergymen, I'm doing it with a beer."

"I took a photo." Elana rummaged in her bag and pulled out her phone. She brought up the picture gallery and flicked through the pictures with her index finger. Mark, Jeff and Sandra all peered over her shoulder.

She stopped on a picture of the moor. "Next one, I think." She pushed her finger up the screen and the next photo slid into view. A panoramic of Dartmoor slid into view. The screen had narrowed to accommodate the photo, so she zoomed in. She scrolled around the photo, but she couldn't find what she was looking for.

"Wait, he was there."

"Pretty poor taste, young lady," Sandra said and went back to the bar.

Elana pointed at the empty horizon in the photo. Hills rolled away and the fading light glowed on the distant Tors. "He was there. He was standing right there."

Chapter 9

Bruce entered the kitchen and paused, leaning on one of the counter tops like he was carrying a heavy weight. The room was small but functional. An enormous fridge freezer dominated the room as it towered over the rest of the equipment. It sat in the middle of wall opposite Bruce. On the adjacent wall, kitchen units ran around the perimeter stopping at a range cooker. Bruce was leaning on a counter that was above a dishwasher that was far too small for the pub. An island in the middle of the room held two more units. A magnetic knife rack was screwed into the wall behind him and pots of utensils dotted the surfaces. Another set of knives sat in a block on the island. Saran had pushed this to the edge as she was using the rest of the island to plate up some food. She didn't look up as Bruce entered.

"You alright?" she asked.

"Where's the wood?"

"The wood?" She picked up two of the plates and looked at him.

"Yeah, the firewood," Bruce said. He was frowning, making him look closer to his actual age.

"I told you earlier," Saran said, turning to the door to the pub.

"Told me what?"

"The guy called – what's his name?" She stopped, head bent in thought.

"Dave."

"Dave, yes that's it," she said with a smile. "He called and said he wouldn't be able to get to us today. Said he'd come over first thing. I told you earlier. Is there a problem?"

Bruce shook his head in exasperation. "You didn't tell me, and yes there's a problem. We've got no wood."

"I did tell you, but it shouldn't matter. There's enough out there for tonight surely."

"No, Saran, there is no wood at all. There's barely even a stick out there."

She put the plates down and looked at him, her mouth open in a perfect 'o' of surprise. "Well, what are we going to do about the fire? It's going to go out."

"Obviously."

"It's burned for one hundred and fifty years and it goes out before we've even owned the pub for a month."

"Yes, yes and then the Devil will appear." Bruce rolled his eyes. "But there's a bigger problem than that. If this snow continues, it's going to get really cold in here."

Saran turned away from him again. She picked up the plates and took them out to the pub. Bruce remained leaning against the work surfaces. He ran his hand through his hair and was still standing like that when Saran returned moments later.

"If we get everyone to a room, they can huddle up in blankets till the morning, then the wood will arrive," she said, giving him a quick hug. "Don't worry, none of them are local, we just won't tell anyone the fire went out. It's bound to have happened before."

Bruce nodded. He'd heard stories of marines pissing on the fire and hot spells where the previous owners had not bothered to light it. *Rumours, though, just rumours.*

"I've just been outside, it's well below freezing already and it's not even eight o'clock." He grimaced. "What's it going to be like at midnight?"

"We'll just have to sleep with our socks on." She pecked his cheek. "Come on, let's go tell everyone the bad news."

James put another pint down in front of Mark. "This'll warm you up." He thought for a moment, then added, "Won't stop you seeing phantom monks though." He chuckled to himself and sat down.

Mark had his arm around Elana, hugging her tight into his shoulder. "Thanks for the beer."

"Yeah, thanks," Elana murmured.

"I didn't get you one," James said. "You've barely touched the last one."

With a tut, Elana raised her glass and took a small sip. The wine was no longer chilled and left a faint metallic taste in her mouth. She forced herself to swallow it with a smile. *One won't hurt.*

Saran arrived and put two plates in front of them. James smiled at her, but she ignored him and returned to the kitchen without a word.

"Fucking lesbian," he muttered with a grin.

Mark laughed at him. "Forget it, mate, she's married."

"Yeah, but he's old enough to be her father."

Elana joined in the laughter, mostly to disguise her disgust at James, but partly to hide her non-drinking. "Don't be daft, he's about five years older than her, and he's pretty fit." She ate a few chips, but the metallic taste remained. Her stomach churned, but it passed quickly.

"What!?" Mark cried in mock indignation.

"Don't worry, honey, he's not got your eyes, but he is cute."

"And I'm not?" James asked, slightly louder than he'd intended.

"To a certain type, no doubt," Mark said.

"Turning gay, Mark?"

"I don't know why I bother talking to you," Elana snapped. She bit into the burger, but her stomach churned again. *Damn.*

"It's my roguish charm." James smiled.

"You're an idiot."

She got up and went to the bar, just as Saran returned with Mark's plate of chips. Elana stopped her with a smile.

"You said about a room," Elana said. "I need a break from that-" she waved a hand at James.

"Yes, I can see why," Saran said. "Let me just put these down." She put the plate in front of Mark. "Come on, I'll show you the rooms."

"What about your food?" Mark called.

Elana shook her head at him, then hurried after Saran.

"Probably wants to be a zero."

"James, for fuck's sake. She really doesn't care about things like that. If you bothered to actually talk to her you'd know that."

"I know her and her sort well enough."

"Do you actually listen to yourself speak?"

"I am wise, like Yoda."

Mark shook his head and munched on his chips. *Maybe she's right. He really is hard work.*

Saran led the way through the door marked 'private'. It led to a corridor that was more of a long thin room than hallway. The kitchen sat directly in front of them and stairs led up at the end of the hall. Wood panelling that wouldn't have looked out of place in a seventies' sitcom lined the walls from floor to ceiling. Two pictures adorned the walls, and Elana was disappointed to see that they were the usual tacky pub ones of dogs playing pool.

"Eventually we'll open this bit up to the public and shut the access to the kitchen off. That way we can do B&B," Saran said. "We'll get rid of these pictures too."

Elana smiled. "I'm glad you said that."

"Oh, it's awful isn't it? This beautiful pub, sorry inn - Bruce gets tetchy if I get it wrong - and you stick up pictures of dogs looking stupid. Who could possibly think these pictures are a good idea?"

Elana laughed out loud for the first time in what felt like hours. "I couldn't agree more."

"Bruce is a good photographer, so we'll decorate everywhere with his photos eventually."

"You might even be able to sell them to gullible tourists."

"We might at that."

Saran led Elana up the steep stairs and out onto a narrow corridor. It was dark as only a single light hung in the middle of the ceiling, its faint glow barely reaching the edges of the carpet.

"Bit dark," Saran said, "sorry. We will also get better lighting up here."

It was beginning to sound all a bit 'we will' to Elana. She couldn't help wondering if it would still look like this if they came back in a year. Lots of people have grand plans – how many actually follow them through?

Three doors led off this corridor, two on the left. Saran opened the door on the right. They were in a large room with a four poster bed. The whole room was very tastefully decorated, with oak furniture and beautiful photographs of Dartmoor on the walls. Saran watched Elana's face as she took in the room.

"Wow."

"This is the only finished one," Saran said. "The other two are decorated, but the furniture needs replacing to get them up to the standard of this one. This will obviously be our expensive room. What do you think?"

Elana nodded. "It's fantastic." She inspected the photos more closely. "He has a good eye. I think you'll definitely be able to sell these."

"There's an ensuite through there with a bath and shower," she pointed at a wooden door in the corner of the room. "I wanted a Jacuzzi bath, but do you know how much they cost?"

Elana nodded again, even though she had no idea.

"Make yourself comfortable. This is your room for the night. I'll put your burger back in the oven, so it'll still be warm when you're ready for it."

"Thanks," Elana said. She had totally forgotten about the food. *Had James pissed me off that much?*

"Towels in the bathroom, spares in the ottoman, if you want to shower."

"Think I will," Elana said, hugging herself. It wasn't warm in the room. "Travelling always makes me feel grubby."

Saran pulled the door shut behind her and Elana heard her heavy footsteps going back down the corridor. She sat on the bed and sank into it. She lay back, leaving her feet dangling over the edge. The bed was firm but comfortable, despite being new. Elana felt her eyes close and –

- she felt a hand run up her leg and she leapt to her feet, a scream dying in her throat. Lips pressed to hers, and a tongue started probing her mouth. She wrestled for a second, then felt hands move onto her buttocks. Familiar, strong hands. She pushed hard on his chest and stepped to the side.

"Jesus, Mark, you scared the shit out of me."

He looked genuinely crestfallen. "Sorry hun, I just thought-"

"What? That you'd scare me awake?"

"No," Mark held up his hands in the universal gesture for calm down. "I didn't know you were asleep. I saw you lying on the bed and-"

"One track mind," Elana said, beginning to smile.

"Cold in here, isn't it?" Mark hugged her, pulling her close to his chest.

"A bit, but I'm glad we're in here." She kissed him on the lips. "I feel better now we're not on the road."

"Me too. It was getting pretty hairy out there."

He let her go and crossed to the window. The curtains were open, showing the thick snow and fog that still passed outside. Mark pressed his face to the glass, cupping his hands around his eyes so he could see.

There was nothing to see. The fog was too thick, although as it swirled it threatened to reveal the moor. The snow was settling everything with a thick blanket of white. *This will not be gone by morning, what happens then? If this snow keeps coming we could be here for days.* Shivering, he turned back to Elana.

She had stripped down to her bra and knickers and had a huge grin on her face. She hooked her thumbs under the shoulder straps and said, "Wanna come warm me up?"

He did.

James sat in the bar, next to the fire, feeling more than a little lonely. He cast the occasional glance at the bar, where Jeff and Sandra were still sitting. They had barely exchanged a word in the last thirty minutes. *Come on Jeff, she's still got it, you should be more attentive than that.*

They were ignoring him and there had been no sign of the geezer who ran the place since the food had arrived. He had gone to get wood, but that had been nearly an hour ago now. The fire was beginning to look a little on the underpowered side; just one log glowing faintly in the grate. *He'd better hurry up, or that fire is going to go out. And then what'll happen? Could be fun with wind-ups to be had.*

Bored, he started tapping his glass, the table, the seat. In his head he sang Iron Maiden's *'Number Of The Beast'* over and over again, drumming along on his makeshift kit.

"Can you stop that please?"

He was so engrossed in his own little world that it took him a second or two to register that Jeff was speaking to him.

"What's that, mate?"

"The tapping. Please stop, it really is quite irritating."

James looked at the man, studying him really for the first time since their arrival in the pub. He was at least fifty, full head of hair, greying at the temples. He had the beer belly of a man who had spent too many nights on real ale, and the skin to match. His eyes were sharp, however, a cold blue that constantly scanned the room as if looking for threats.

Afraid he's losing his wife. She's kept her looks, whilst his are slipping and he's terrified of her buggering off. James filed the thought: it could come in handy later if Jeff continued to be an annoying cunt.

James held his hands in the air to show that he was going to stop tapping and sank back to the chair. He put his feet on the table and sank a little lower. *Where the fuck is Mark? What kind of road trip is this? He went to check an Elana over half hour ago, should be back by now.* James shook his head. *Must be getting some. Can't blame him, Elana is well fit, even if more than a little irritating.*

He stood and studied the photos on the wall of days gone by. In one, a helicopter was coming in to land on a snow covered field. The date was in the fifties. *That's a lot of snow.* He glanced at the window. Someone had closed the curtains at some point, and so he lifted one to the side and peered into the gloom. At first he could see nothing but the mist swirling and large flakes of snow. Then-

A man could be seen on the other side of the road, staring straight at him.

"Shit!" James cried, dropping the curtain and falling back from the window. He knocked a table, which in turn pushed a chair backwards. He stood shaking for a moment before picking the chair up.

"Make more noise why don't you?" Jeff said, contempt on his face.

"There's a man out there!"

"Nice try, son, but we've been here before."

Sandra put a hand on his arm as he stood, causing her arm to drop. A look of disappointment crossed her features momentarily, before she seemed to remember where she was and she forced herself to smile.

James stumbled in his attempt to run to the door and he yanked it open. Cold wind howled around him, but he stepped out anyway. "Hey!" His voice disappeared on the wind. "HEY!"

No answer except the wind. The mist continued its swirl in front of his face, rare patches giving him a glimpse of the other side of the road.

The figure remained standing stock still. The hood hid his face, but James could see enough to know that the figure was big. Over six foot and with the build of a prop forward. The man – if it was a man - oozed menace.

"HEY!" James shouted again, although now he was unsure that he wanted an answer. It was bitterly cold, but the man was not moving. The inclination of the hood seemed – *No. Bollocks. I'm not doing this. There is no way he is staring at me.*

"Close the door, for God's sake, it's freezing in here." Jeff grabbed his arm, making him jump.

"That guy," James managed to say, giving Jeff a wild eyed stare. "A monk."

"What guy?" Jeff looked across the road, but could see nothing through the mist. "You're just trying to wind us up, like the others."

"You saw one earlier."

"Yeah, and he's long home by now. Anyone out in this is just going to keel over before too much longer." Jeff turned back to the pub. "Now close the fucking door before we all freeze."

The shock of the older man swearing at him brought James back to his current situation. He was shivering (although it wasn't just the cold making those muscles tremble) and he returned to the warmth of the bar.

He sat back at the table in front of the fire and rubbed his hands together. The fire was now looking more than a little pathetic. The last log was nearly gone. Where was Bruce with that wood?

"Why are they here? What are they doing? Are they trying to scare us?"

He turned to see Sandra shouting at her husband. Jeff gave her a hug, but he remained distant from her: the hug was only with his arms, not his body. Her face was contorted with real fear.

"Relax," he said. "He's just playing games with you."

"I'm really not."

"Shut it, arsehole, you're not helping."

"Jeff."

"No, I'm sick of his little comments and mind games. All of them. It's pathetic. We saw a monk going for a walk on the moor and now everyone's seeing monks everywhere. Truly pathetic."

"I know what I saw."

"And I saw nothing," Jeff said through gritted teeth. "There's nobody out there, and if there were, they'd be freezing to death."

"But they saw them. We saw them. What do they want?" Sandra's voice was high and shrill.

"Nothing. They're not there. There's nobody outside this pub – look at the weather for God's sake."

"Don't blaspheme."

"Oh, for Christ's sake woman." Jeff rolled his eyes. "Are you scared or are you worried about my vocabulary? I've had enough of this."

"Where're you going to go?" James asked, with a smirk.

"What?"

"Take a look outside Jeff. None of us are leaving tonight, it's carnage out there."

"Carnage out there," Jeff mimicked. "Wipe that smirk off your face sunshine, you look simple. Don't speak to me or her again tonight, alright? Just leave us alone." He turned his back to James and hunched over his pint at the bar. His shoulders remained taut and his mouth was a thin line of anger.

"What if-"

"Sandra, no love, just leave it."

"But Jeff-"

"There are no mad monks out there watching the pub. It's ludicrous. Why on earth would they watch this dump anyway?"

Bruce chose that exact moment to reappear behind the bar. Jeff blushed slightly but didn't say anymore, though it was clear that Bruce had heard him.

"I apologise for my husband," Sandra said, though whether she was talking to James or Bruce was unclear.

"Yeah, I feel for you," James said. He took in Bruce's empty hands. "What's up, couldn't find any trees to chop down?"

Bruce looked at his feet, then ran his hand through his hair. "Sorry, um, we've got a slight problem with the wood."

"I'll bet you do," James muttered.

"We seem to have run out. The guy was supposed to deliver today, but obviously with the snow, he couldn't get out to us."

"I'm sure the heating will keep us warm," Sandra said. Her voice was more normal now; she was calming down, trying not to think of why some monks would brave this weather to watch a rundown old pub.

"Well, now," Bruce started.

"What do you mean, 'well now'?" Jeff was displaying a lot of skill at mimicry.

"Let him speak, for fuck's sake," James said.

"Let's all calm down shall we?" Bruce said.

"I'll calm down when you explain what you mean," Jeff snarled.

"I was about to, but you didn't really give me a chance."

Saran re-entered the bar at that moment. "What's with the shouting?"

"Listen, it's ok, we've just run out of wood," Bruce said. "The problem is that the fire runs our boiler."

"That's just great," Jeff said.

James crossed the bar, slamming his pint glass down with more force than he'd intended. "What are you talking about? What does that even mean? The fire run our boiler?"

"The system here is really old. Basically the fire powers our boiler which in turn gives us heat throughout the pub. It's a great system really."

"Unless the fire goes out," Jeff said.

"Yes," Bruce agreed.

"Right, so when that log stops burning we have no heat in this building?" James said.

"Right."

"I don't want to worry anyone, but have you seen the weather outside?"

"This is a cob building. We'll be ok."

"What the hell is cob?"

"Thick walls basically. Pretty good insulation."

"If it's hot in here already."

Bruce said nothing to that.

"What are we going to do?" Sandra asked. Her voice remained calm; it seemed to James that she was more worried about the monks than the very real possibility of them freezing overnight.

"Cut up the furniture."

"You can't do that!" Bruce said. "I can't afford to get any more!"

Saran held up calming hands. "You've all got rooms, with thick duvets in them. We can get more blankets and everyone stay in bed until morning."

"Three rooms," James said. "But there's seven of us."

"Bruce and I have a house next door. We'll go there."

"Your house? That will have heating," Sandra said. "We should all go there now."

Saran shook her head. "No, the house is connected to the pub with heating and the generators. We're going to have central heating fitted soon." She smiled at them all. "If it gets really, really cold we could all cuddle up."

"Great if you've got someone to cuddle up to," James muttered.

"Nobody thinks you're funny," Jeff said.

"Actually, that's not true. My mum thinks I'm hilarious."

"What about the story?" Sandra said suddenly.

"The story?" Bruce looked blank.

"The one that awful man said."

"Oh, for God's sake," Jeff said. "What is wrong with you?"

Bruce was still looking blank, so Saran helped him out. "You know the legend about the fire?"

"Oh, that!" Bruce smiled. "Adam was just pulling your leg, don't worry."

"What story?" James asked.

"There is a legend-"

"Story," Bruce interjected with a smirk at his wife.

"Legend," she continued with a firmer tone, "that the fire has burned here for over two hundred years. The ashes were carried over from the old building and the fire set."

"So?" James looked unimpressed. "Usual tourist bullshit tale."

"My, my, we agree on something," Jeff muttered.

"Well, the old building burnt down because an old gambler had angered the devil. The gambler, what was his name?"

Bruce shrugged. "Can't remember."

"It doesn't matter. The gambler tried to trick the devil, but he came to get him anyway. The gambler set a fire in the pub to keep the devil out, but the fire spread and he had to run outside. The devil collected him and flew away with him, making the gambler drop the four aces he had hidden up his sleeves. You can still see the cards on the moor side now."

"There is so much wrong with that story," James said.

"Mostly the fact that you can't see the cards on the hillside," Bruce said. "I've looked. If you squint you can see a diamond, but it could just be a square field on the hillside. Saran reckons she can see the spade, but I'm not convinced. It's a good story though."

"The cards on the moor is your *biggest* problem?" James said.

"Well-"

"How about scaring away the Devil with fire? That's like trying to keep Jordan away with paparazzi."

"Who?" Jeff asked.

James and Bruce both shook their heads. "Man, you are older than you look," James said. "Also, who ever heard of the Devil flying?"

"If you believe in the Devil," Jeff said, "then you believe a lot of crazy shit."

"Stop swearing," Sandra said. "It makes you sound common."

"What's going to happen? The Devil gonna get me?" Jeff shook his arms and body like a child doing an impression of a ghost.

"Jeff!"

That was when the screaming started.

Chapter 10

The shower was hot and surprisingly powerful. The water bounced off their bodies as they kissed.

"I enjoyed that," Elana said, her face still flushed. She rubbed soap over his chest and thighs, pausing for a second until he groaned. "Still a bit of life then!" She dropped to her knees, no easy feat in the cramped shower, kissing his body as she went. The hot water running over his head intensified the feelings until he came again.

She stood up, grinning and wiping her mouth with the back of her hand. He kissed her cheek and hugged her.

"I love you."

"What?" she said. The noise of the water nearly drowned out her voice even though she was close to his ear.

"I love you." A little louder this time.

"Can't hear you over this water, what did you say?"

He punched her playfully on the shoulder. "You heard."

"Love you too," she said, still grinning. "I'm going to get dry."

She got out of the shower, leaving him to enjoy the spray a little longer. Mark sagged against the wall of the cubicle. Elana took some keeping up with when she was in that sort of mood. He shampooed his hair and washed his body with shower gel. *Energiser, my arse.* The water had just started to cool down when he heard the screams.

Elana dried herself quickly. It was cold in the room now, a sure sign that the temperature outside was falling fast. Still, *it will be nice and warm down in the bar with the fire.* She wrapped the towel around herself and looked through her bag. She found clean underwear and a top and laid them out on the bed next to her jeans and thick jumper. Her hair was still dripping wet, with small rivulets running down her shoulders and back.

She pulled everything out of her bag, but couldn't find her hairdryer. *Typical.* Maybe this room had one - it was being prepared for a B&B after all. She opened the wardrobe, but it was empty apart from a few of the hangers you usually saw in Travelodges and Holiday Inns that only fit the bar they came from. She smiled to herself. Clearly Bruce and Saran were concerned about people stealing their clothes hangers. She closed the wardrobe and started to root through the chest of drawers.

Also empty. *Damn it, I'm going to freeze with this wet hair.* She saw the ottoman at the foot of the bed and opened it. The lid creaked open and she saw some old linen trousers and a pair of ancient hob nailed boots. They were covering the lower half of a body. Her eyes drifted up the body and her breath caught in her throat. A thick moth-eaten woollen jumper clothed the top half of the body. *No hands, he's got no hands.* Two open eyes stared out at her, pupils wide and unstaring. Black hair hung limp over a pale face. The lips were parted slightly, but no breath came out of them.

Elana started to scream.

Mark leapt out of the shower and ran into the bedroom, leaving a trail of wet footprints behind him. The cold air instantly made him shiver, but in his urgency he didn't care. Elana was standing in the corner of the bedroom, towel wrapped around her, hand on mouth. She was shaking and pointing at the ottoman.

"What?" Mark yelled.

"There's," she paused, trying to stop the tremor in her voice. "There's a corpse in the ottoman at the foot of my bed."

He hugged her tightly. "Jesus."

He turned to look at the ottoman. The lid had dropped shut when Elana had started screaming. He took a step towards it. *I've seen horror films that start like this. Oh crap, oh crap. Bruce and Saran are surely far too nice to be a couple of psychos.*

"Mark," Elana held his arm. "Don't."

"It'll be fine," he said. His stomach did a flip and he felt removed from his body for a second. He could see the room from the ceiling: Elana shivering in the corner, wet hair plastered to her exquisite shoulders; the unfamiliar room tastefully furnished for guests who would never visit; the new furniture stylishly blending with the surroundings and the ottoman standing at the foot of the bed. He watched himself cross to the ottoman, each tentative step taking him closer to the box.

He snapped back to his body to find that he was standing next to the ottoman. He heard footsteps rushing up the stairs as he lifted the lid. Empty eyes stared back up at him and he threw the lid back so that it banged on the wooden frame of the bed. The door burst open behind him, but he ignored the new arrivals. For no reason he could really explain he reached out and touched the corpse, and then started laughing.

"It's *'Carry On Screaming'*," James said from the doorway, smirking at Mark's bare bottom.

"What's going on?" Bruce asked. "Is everyone ok?" Then he saw the ottoman, and his expression softened. To Mark, it looked like someone fearing the worst, being given good news instead. "I see you've found Derek."

"Derek?" Elana shouted. "What-"

Mark went to her quickly and gave her a hug. "It's a dummy."

"What?"

"It's a dummy. It's not a corpse, it's a shop dummy, like you know..." he searched for the right word, "a mannequin."

"Dude, put some clothes on," James said, as Sandra and Saran joined them in the doorway.

Mark stepped behind Elana, turning red in the process. "Um, sorry. James, man, can you throw me a towel from the bathroom?"

"Sure, if it means I don't have to see your spotty arse again."

"False alarm folks," Bruce said, smiling like a used car salesman. "Elana, I'm sorry Derek gave you such a shock."

"Who is Derek?" Sandra asked.

"The dummy." Bruce pointed at the ottoman.

Now she looked more closely, Elana could see the plastic sheen of the skin on the face and she turned as red as Mark.

"Sorry everyone," she said. "I feel like such an idiot."

"Why have you got a dummy stuffed in an ottoman anyway?" James asked. He had handed Mark a towel and was now inspecting the dummy closely.

"It's another tourist story I'm afraid," Bruce said. "Story goes that a man died here years back, and they kept the body stored in salt to slow the decomposition until the doctor could get here. Someone stayed in the room and, well, the outcome was similar to this."

"We thought it would be a good idea to play on the myths associated with this place more than the previous owners did." Saran said. "I'm sorry we shocked you, Elana, are you ok?"

She nodded. "Nothing hurt but my pride. It's so obvious it's a dummy isn't it?"

Nobody nodded except James.

"Uh, could we have some privacy please?" Mark said. He had wrapped the towel around his waist, but there were still traces of water on his body, making him cold. He was grateful that he had put on enough weight recently that you could no longer count his ribs, but he still wished he was more toned.

"Certainly," Bruce said. Jeff and Sandra left first, Jeff trying hard not to notice the look Sandra threw at Mark, and they were followed closely by the owners. James smirked at Elana and Mark.

"Naughty, naughty." He leered at Elana.

"Go away, James, you, you-" Elana paused, searching for the right word, "-child."

"Good one, Els," James said, "that covered all the bases. Witty, insightful and oh so cutting. I'll be back at the bar, sobbing into my beer, wondering where it all went wrong if you need me."

Mark slammed the door after pushing him out into the corridor. "Honestly, why are you friends with him?"

"We went to school together, come on," Mark said, hugging her, partly to make her feel better but mostly to warm himself up. "We've been mates since we were about five."

"Yes, and if you met now, would you be friends at all?"

"That's a ridiculous thing to say."

"No it's not. If you met now you'd have nothing in common. You'd think he was a prize idiot."

"He's not that bad. You just need to get to know him."

I have, Elana nearly said, but stopped herself just in time. *No need for Mark to know about that, no need at all.* She had planned to give Mark the other news when they had some privacy, but the moment had passed for now. Though she could see the 'dead body' was clearly a shop dummy, something about the situation had deeply unnerved her.

They got dressed quickly and in a comfortable silence. At some point Mark closed the ottoman lid, which made her feel better. Mark had put his Ben Sherman shirt and jeans back on and was reaching for his glasses. Elana smiled at him; he always looked at his best straight after a shower whilst his dark hair was almost black from the water and his blue eyes sparkled.

"You set?" he asked. Her stomach somersaulted and she knew then that this would be the man she would marry.

"Set."

James sat at the bar, two beers and Elana's vodka in front of him. He drank heavily from one of the pints and then looked at Jeff and Sandra. *What brought them to this stage of marriage?* Sandra, glamorous and the dictionary definition of 'still got it'. Jeff, the same dictionary's definition of 'let himself go' with his beer belly, jowls and grey hair. *Clooney he is not.*

"What are you looking at city boy?" Jeff snarled.

"Jeff," Sandra said, "stop being so obnoxious."

"He's undressing you with his eyes."

"For Pete's sake, I'm old enough to be his mother."

Yep, a proper MILF. "I'm not from the city."

"What?"

"You seem to be judging me on being a 'city boy'. You know what they say about people who assume."

"You look like one of those city traders to me."

"What do you mean by that?"

"All flash, no substance. Into your cars and bloody mobile phones aren't you?"

"Yeah, but that doesn't make me flash. It makes me under thirty-five, granddad."

"So, what do you do James?" Sandra asked. Her tone was light, the same as his parents used whenever he brought an unsuitable girlfriend home.

"I'm a teacher. Head of department actually."

"It's Friday. Shouldn't you be at work?" Jeff asked. It seemed to James that his voice had softened slightly – the teacher card often changed people's preconceptions about him.

James looked at his watch. "Nah, school's out till Monday." He sang the words like Alice Cooper.

"That other fella made it sound like you'd been travelling for hours."

"We have. I took a little personal time." James winked at Sandra.

"So you let down all those kids today, because you wanted a jolly?" Jeff's snarl was back.

"Ahh, can it, old man. You know nothing about me."

"Long may it stay that way."

Bruce returned to the bar, carrying a large axe. He rested it against the bar, near the till. He beamed as Mark and Elana re-entered the bar. They returned his smile, ruefully, and then sat by the fire. James stayed at the bar.

"How we doing here?" Bruce asked.

"Just dandy," James said, earning yet another scowl from Jeff.

"We're fine, thank you." Sandra said. Behind her, the fire sputtered.

"Fire's going out," Jeff observed.

"Great, maybe the Devil will come, liven things up around here," James said.

"You shouldn't joke about such things," Sandra said.

"Ah, come on." James stood up, taking the two pints (although one was far nearer a half now) with him. He put the full pint in front of Mark without a word and crossed to the window. Stopping in front of the window, he pulled the curtain back. Thick fog obscured the view out of the window and the complete black of night added to the oppressiveness. An occasional snow flake broke the wall of white, the different shade of white surprisingly clear against the fog. He cupped his hands around his eyes and pressed his face against the glass. His breath fogged on the pane.

"If the devil's coming, love, he'd better be wearing a warm coat," James said loudly. As he watched, shadows coalesced in the distances – how far away was too hard to tell because of the fog. More than one loomed in the strange combination of dark and light caused by night and the fog.

"What are you talking about?" Mark said.

James filled him in with a brief version of the tale of the gambler and the Devil he heard earlier.

"Load of old bollocks, right?" James resumed staring out of the window.

Something was moving out there, something too big to be an animal.

"What the hell?" James said, more quietly this time. He opened the door to the outside and cold wind once more swept into the bar. The fire flared briefly, but it was a futile effort; it was going out quickly.

"What the hell are you doing now, boy?"

"James?" Sandra's voice trembled as she spoke. *Did she really believe the story? Jesus, some people.*

"There's definitely something moving out here," James said. Mark suddenly appeared at his side.

"What are you doing? You're letting all the heat out."

"Mark, you've seen it. There's something out here. I saw it earlier, but that knobhead didn't believe me."

"It'll be a horse, or a deer or something. Come on, back inside."

"Hang on. He's not getting away this time." He stepped out of the porch, onto the road. Thick snow crunched underfoot. No danger of a car suddenly appearing and mowing him down. He kept his eyes fixed on what he assumed was the other side of the road. He thought he could see dark shadows lined up on that side. More than one.

"Guys, come on," Bruce's voice made Mark jump. He had followed James into the road without realising it.

"It's cold," Bruce continued.

"No shit," James muttered. He hadn't taken his eyes off the spot ahead, on the other side of the road. Mark followed his gaze. Was that movement? He squinted just as a snow flake landed on his eyelash. The snow was slowing down, which was a relief. Maybe they would be able to get out of here in the morning after all.

A shadow was clearly defined against the fog. Standing roughly five metres away was a large dark shape, with its edges indistinct against the fog. It was roughly man shaped, but a very large man. The fog cleared as James shouted something Mark didn't catch.

"What?" Mark shouted.

James turned and bumped into him. The breath was knocked out of Mark and he doubled over. James didn't apologise, didn't stop. He was moving back inside the pub as quickly as the snow would allow.

"James?" Mark sputtered. He looked up just as the fog cleared. Twelve monks stood at the edge of the road in a rough semi-circle. All heads were bowed, faces shrouded in darkness. A low sound was coming from the monks. They were chanting. Even at this short distance, the dampening effects of the fog made it difficult to hear what they were chanting.

The sound chilled Mark to the bone. Fear welled inside him; the chant hit him in some primal part of his brain that he didn't need to understand. He needed to flee.

"Come on." Bruce put his hand on his shoulder. Mark screamed. Actually screamed; a sound he hadn't thought he could make until three seconds ago.

Mark's scream seemed to break the chant. One of the monks looked up at them. He raised his hand and pointed at them. *No, not at us. He's pointing at the pub.*

"He is coming," the monk said.

"What do you want?" Bruce shouted, but the monks had resumed their chanting. "You'll die out here."

Mark pushed Bruce back towards the pub. "They're not listening. Come on."

"We can't just leave them."

"Yes, we fucking well can." Fear had gripped Mark completely. His legs felt like jelly, but he forced himself to walk. They got back to the pub and Bruce locked the door behind them.

Saran was frowning from the door of the kitchen. Everyone else was staring at the door.

"What do they want?" Sandra shouted. "What do they want?"

"Calm down," Jeff said.

"Did you hear them?" Sandra was on the verge of hysterics.

Elana went to Mark. "What's going on?" she asked quietly and he loved her even more for how calm she appeared.

"I have no idea." He wanted to explain the irrational fear that had gripped him outside. A bunch of monks chanting in the snow. *Get a grip Mark.*

-He is coming-

"I think we should make sure the fire keeps going," Bruce muttered.

"Great idea," James said. He was back at the bar, having reclaimed his pint enroute. His hand shook as he drank.

"Wait, you're not serious?" Elana asked. She looked at Mark, searching his face for some clue as to James' sudden change of heart.

"Couldn't harm," Mark said. He smiled at Elana. "At least we'll stay warm."

75

Bruce went to the bar and picked up his large axe.

"Bruce, wait, the furniture isn't paid for yet," Saran said.

"Right now, I don't care." Bruce went to the nearest empty table and swung the axe. The table smashed on the second go, a satisfying crack splitting it into two halves.

-he is coming-

"Bruce," Mark said, looking at the fire. Everyone stopped and followed his gaze.

The fire had gone out.

Part Three: The Devil's In.

"Why would I want some vestal virgin? How dull are they?"

Chapter 11

"The fire!" Sandra shrieked.

"Oh for God's sake," Jeff said.

"Don't panic!" Bruce said.

"Everybody be quiet!" Mark shouted.

Elana and Saran said nothing: they were staring at the door.

"Quiet!" Mark shouted again.

"It's just a fire," Jeff said, rolling his eyes.

"I need a beer," James said. Mark shot him a look that made James shrug. Now back in the warmth of the pub, in the safety of something so familiar, some of James' machismo had returned.

Tap. Tap. Tap.

They all exchanged glances.

"Someone is knocking on the door," Elana said. She hadn't taken her eyes from the door since the moment the fire went out.

"Someone outside," Saran agreed.

"Well they wouldn't be knocking from the inside," James said, earning himself another stern look from Mark.

"Don't open it!" Sandra said.

"Why not?" Jeff asked. "Somebody is knocking on the door of a pub. Let them in."

"What if it's one of those monks?" James asked.

"Maybe they're getting cold," Jeff said.

"You weren't outside just now," Bruce said. Mark nodded.

Elana looked at Mark, seeking clues on his face. His brow was creased, and his mouth turned down as it always did when he was concentrating. He was definitely worried about something. What's up? She mouthed, but he shook his head once, his frown increasing.

"What's happened?" Saran asked.

Bruce glanced at the other two men, looking for help. "I don't know. There's more of them. It was weird."

"Weird how?"

-He is coming-

Bruce said nothing and Mark shivered.

Tap. Tap. Tap.

Louder now.

"Why are you worried?" Jeff asked, sliding his hand through his thinning hair. "Go open the door."

"The fire's gone out!" Sandra said. Her voice was no calmer and she was very pale.

"So fucking what?" Jeff snarled. "It's just a story."

Sandra flinched at her husband's swearing but said nothing. Jeff stood up and made a move to the door. James stepped forward and put a hand on his chest.

"Don't," James said.

"Get off me, city boy." Jeff brushed James' hand aside. They stood toe to toe for a second, staring at each other, neither man moving.

"You don't know what's on the other side of that door."

Jeff laughed, a sound that was just wrong in the bar. He looked at the group, taking in the frowns and pale faces. "You lot have lost the plot. A fire goes out and you've all become more hysterical than a group of school girls at a pop concert. Pathetic." He saved his most withering look for Sandra. "I am so surprised at you."

"I'm warning you," James said.

"What?" Jeff continued to laugh. "You're warning me because I'm going to open a door and let someone who is probably freezing into the warm. Honestly, get out of my way."

"James," Mark called and shook his head once.

"This is a mistake," James said. "It might not be a story."

"Seriously?" Elana asked. "You think that the Devil has turned up because a fire has gone out?"

James said nothing so Jeff stepped past him, shooting Elana a look of thanks. He walked to the door and it seemed that time slowed down. Each step stretched like slow motion in a film. His hand reached out for the lock, an old fashioned slide bolt at the top of the door which looked like a good shove would break it anyway.

Mark realised he was holding his breath as he heard the lock slide back. He strode over to Jeff and stood next to him. He was surprised to see that Jeff did look nervous: the atmosphere in the room had got to him after all.

"It's just a fire, right?" Mark said.

"Right," Jeff said and opened the door.

A dark figure fell through the door and landed at Mark's feet. Almost immediately, the figure curled into the foetal position and Mark knew it wasn't one of the weird monks. Dark jeans and a well-worn pair of working boots clad the lower half; a coat with a strange pattern on it adorned the outer half. He bent closer to examine the pattern. A care label was visible and under one arm could be seen a Harrington label. The coat was inside out.

"Who is it?" The shrill voice came from the other side of the bar and Mark didn't need to look to know who had spoken.

"Christ, he's half frozen," Jeff muttered, ignoring his considerably better half.

Pale eyes looked at Jeff, then closed. "So cold." The voice was faint.

"Blankets," Mark said to Jeff, then louder for everyone's benefit. "We need blankets and hot water, now!"

Saran and Elana ran – actually ran – through the door to the service area. They returned moments later carrying a bundle of blankets each. Jeff and Mark lifted the figure and carried him gently over to the fire place. Smoke still rose up the chimney, tendrils escaping in to the room occasionally, and the residual heat was still strong.

"Warmer than outside anyway," Mark said, putting the man in one of the chairs that Jeff had dragged closed to the fireplace.

"Bruce, he's going to need the fire," Mark said to the landlord. "Also, it's got a lot colder outside, we're going to need the extra warmth too."

Bruce seemed on the verge of arguing, not being entirely happy with being told what to do in his own pub, but he nodded. "I don't really like these tables anyway." He hefted the axe with a grin.

James and Sandra edged closer to the man, and the cluster of strangers around him.

"Is that-?" Sandra asked.

"Yes." Jeff nodded gravely; behind him, Bruce was smashing up one of the tables. "It's the man who attacked me."

"So cold," Adam said again. He opened his eyes and looked from Jeff to James. His whole body was shivering and he hugged the blankets tighter around him.

"It'll be alright, Adam," Saran said, putting a light hand on his shoulder.

"Jesus, Adam," Bruce said. "We thought you'd gone home."

"Yeah, dude, you should be at home," James said.

"Home?" Adam glared at him. "I've only just arrived."

"No, earlier. What did you think you were doing, coming back out in this?"

"I got things to say to that guy." Adam pointed at Jeff, who found that he could not return the stare.

"Say something Jeff," Sandra said. Her voice seemed to have returned to normal now; the sight of a familiar face served to calm her down.

"Yes, Jeff, say something," Adam said, but he was looking at Sandra.

"He hasn't apologised yet," Jeff said, spreading his arms wide.

"Are you ok?" Mark asked Adam, ignoring Jeff and his childish protestations.

Adam didn't move his gaze from Jeff. "You're first." He pointed at Jeff.

"First for what?"

"First for the apology!" Sandra said. "For God's sake Jeff, what's got into you?"

"Don't be profane," Jeff spat, but he still said nothing to Adam. Sandra's eyes welled up and she turned from everyone in the room. Elana went to her and put her arm around her shoulders. Elana looked at Jeff, contempt clear in her eyes.

"Hurry with that wood, Bruce," Adam said, finally shifting his gaze from Jeff. "And you, something to eat." He glared at Saran.

"Adam, if you weren't half frozen I'd bar you again," Bruce said.

"It's fine," Saran said, "I can get him a coffee."

Mark sat next to Adam. "We're going to get the fire going, as soon as Bruce is ready. It'll get a lot warmer in here then."

"Natural leader huh?" Adam said. "Interesting."

Mark shook his head and laughed. "No, not at all, just trying to keep the peace. Jeff's not that bad you know." The lie came easy, and later he would wonder about that. "You warmer?" Something about Adam's voice was niggling away at the back of Mark's mind.

Adam nodded, but the expression on his face remained that of a man who had sucked the sting out of a wasp. "Hurry, it's not enough."

Mark left him and went to Bruce. As he crossed the bar, he saw Elana sit Sandra at one of the tables and smiled at her. James passed in front of him, blocking the smile and Elana sat down without even seeing Mark. James sat next to her, almost on top of her really, and put his arm casually across the back of her seat. Elana threw him a smile but continued to comfort Sandra. Mark paused for a second. *Now what is this?* As the thought flashed across his mind, he felt a flush on his cheeks that wasn't heat. His stomach knotted: *you're my best friend.*

"Give us a hand," Bruce said, breaking his reverie. He was holding a pile of wood, sweat trickling down the side of his face.

"Sure." Mark took the wood back to the fire and started arranging it in the grate. He looked over his shoulder at Adam. "Fire's coming."

Bruce brought the rest of the wood over, expertly ripped up some newspaper and a fire was roaring in the grate moments later. The thick smell of wood smoke filled the room, reminding Mark of childhood Christmases. Bruce went back to the bar and Mark lingered, throwing Adam a smile that said: *see, fire's going, soon be warm.*

"Are you comfortable with that?" Adam asked, his face suddenly close to Mark's ear.

"With what?" Mark asked, snapping his gaze back to Adam. He recoiled slightly as he saw the pale eyes studying him intently.

"Those two. Thick as thieves like that."

"I'm not sure what you're getting at there." Mark tried to laugh, but it died in his throat. "That's my best friend and my girlfriend."

"Trust him do you?"

"Trust him?" *Well that's the question isn't it?* James had been known to move in on girls in the past, but that was usually during the chatting up phase, not the actual going out. *Boys' code of honour, he called it.* More importantly, Mark trusted Elana.

"Look at him, Mark, take a good look. Your best mate is moving in on your girl whilst you're trying to be nice to a stranger."

"You're wrong," Mark said, but his stomach did another flip. "She loves me."

"Yes, but James is better looking than you. He's more fun, a little bit of a bad boy. All the girls love a bad boy."

Mark stood up suddenly. "What the fuck is wrong with you? You know nothing about her or me." *But he got James right didn't he?*

"I know that she's sucked his cock."

"What?" Mark felt like he'd been punched in the stomach and sat down quickly.

"In a night club whilst you were away."

"Shut the fuck up," Mark said. "What the hell is wrong with you?"

"It's true. Ask him. He was bragging about it earlier, whilst you were upstairs. I heard it through the window."

"How-"

"Mmm, yeah," Adam threw back his head, raising his hand to imitate a blow job. "He was big, far bigger than *you*. She could barely fit him in her mouth." Adam lent in towards Mark, like they were old confidants. "It made her so wet she even let him come all over her face."

"You're full of shit. Fuck off." Mark stood again, anger pulsing through him like a wave. Why had he even listened to this twat of a man who couldn't possibly know these things?

"Ask him Mark," Adam smiled. "Or even better ask her."

Mark strode across the bar, heading for them. James stood as he approached and Mark noticed that his arm dropped from around her shoulders as he did so. With a roar, Mark drew back his fist and drove it straight into James's nose with as much force as he could muster. An audible crack filled the sudden silence in the bar.

"Mark!" Elana screamed as James fell back over the chair he had risen from. He sprawled across the floor of the pub and Mark jumped on him raining punches down on James's head. Several connected, but most hit James' arms. He lay foetal on the floor, arms over his head as he shouted, "Stop! Stop!"

"Mark!" Elana shouted again, trying to grab his hands. Mark whirled around and pushed her away from him."

"You've sucked his cock!"

"What?" James said, his voice muffled by blood and swelling.

"You gave him a blow job in a nightclub."

Elana said nothing, but she wasn't looking at him.

"Tell me it's not true," Mark heard his voice break, felt tears well in his eyes.

"What the fuck, Mark-" James said.

"It was years ago," Elana said, quietly. "Years before I met you."

"What?" James asked.

Tears now rolled down Mark's face. "How could you?" he said. Everyone else in the bar tried to look away, but this was turning into a live action version of car crash TV: you couldn't look away, no matter how much you wanted to. Adam watched with barely contained glee on his face.

"I didn't even know you then. I was eighteen!"

"Eighteen?" Mark looked confused.

"I'd just gone to Uni. I was so young." She burst into tears and Sandra tried to put her arm around her, but Elana shook it off. Mark stared at Adam, who returned his gaze with his pale eyes drinking in the other man's discomfort.

"What are you talking about?" James asked, sitting up. Saran handed him some kitchen roll and he dabbed at his nose, wincing as he did so.

"You don't remember do you?" Elana said. "After all this time, you don't even remember me."

Wheels started to turn in Mark's mind, tumblers falling into place. Elana had never liked James, not from day one and this was why: a drunken fling years before, that James didn't even remember.

"You chatted me up in a nightclub in Swansea. I was so flattered." Elana's tears and sobs made it hard to understand what she was saying.

"So flattered that you gave me a blow job?" James looked confused. Then his expression changed, the penny dropping with an almost audible clang. "That was *you*?"

"Fuck." Mark sat heavily in a chair, his head in his hands. "I don't believe this."

His head was filled with memories. Third year of university, James had proposed a trip to Swansea. Sun, surf and sweet women, was how he'd sold it. A bunch of them hired a minibus for the weekend. Mark had got a stomach bug the night before they left and had been forced to cancel, spending the whole weekend near a toilet instead. The stories they came back with; the tales they had told. How he had laughed at the 'blow job' story.

His girlfriend.

The girl he was going to ask to marry him.

"Mark, I didn't know how to tell you."

"Jesus," James actually laughed, "that was you?"

"Shut the fuck up James," Mark said. He balled his fists but then forced them to unclench. His mind whirled around a constant image of Elana on her knees, smiling, in front of James who was slowly unbuckling his trousers. Mark slammed his fist on the table, making everyone jump.

"How did you know?" James asked, looking at Adam. The other man shrugged.

"Mark, I'm so sorry," Elana said.

"Come on, dude, it was years ago. I didn't even remember her." James said. He had managed to stop the flow of blood, but the swelling on his nose wouldn't go down for days. "You got me good, but let's leave it, eh?"

"Don't talk to me," Mark said, pointing at James. "Just… fucking… don't."

Elana moved to sit next to Mark, taking his hands in hers. He didn't pull away, but the tension was clear in the set of his shoulders. "I didn't know you then. I'm sorry I didn't tell you, but how could I? I was ashamed."

"You should have found a way."

"I know, but like I said, I was ashamed. I meet this great guy and turns out his best mate is someone I'd-"

"Don't say it." Mark said, and he let her hands go.

"We hadn't even met when."

"You lied to me."

"I didn't."

"You misled me, then."

"Not intentionally Mark. I-"

"Just leave me alone."

"Mark-" Fresh tears rolled down her cheeks.

"Please." His eyes had welled up again and she had never seen him look so forlorn.

Elana stood up and her eyes met James'.

"Why did you tell him?" James asked.

"I didn't. He did." She jerked a thumb at Adam, who still looked highly amused.

"That's who I meant. Why the fuck would you tell him?"

"I didn't."

"He heard you bragging about it," Mark said. James heard the anger and knew that things had changed between them forever.

"Bragging?" James looked confused. "Until she said, I didn't even remember it."

Mark just stared at him, hatred clear in his expression. "Don't lie."

"I'm not." James looked at the others, his gaze resting on Jeff.

"He didn't say anything of the sort to me," Jeff said. He was frowning as if trying to remember where he'd left his keys that morning.

"Mark, I swear to you I didn't tell a soul," James said. "Like I said, and I'm not proud of this by the way, but I didn't remember it was her."

Slowly, Elana turned to look at Adam. She felt everyone else do the same until all eyes rested on the man in the corner. A low sound emanated from him, and it took her a moment to recognise it as laughter.

"Hello, everybody!" Adam gave a little wave, much like royalty in a carriage. "Can you guess my name?"

Mark felt his mouth drop open. *His voice. His voice is different. He's lost his accent. This is impossible, surely?* "You're full of-"

"Careful, Marky Mark, you need to understand what you're dealing with."

"This is ridiculous," Jeff said. "You're mad."

"Maybe a little," Adam nodded.

"You're Adam Warren," Bruce stuttered. "You've been a regular here since we took over the pub."

"No, Bruce, I *was* Adam, now I'm-" Adam paused, looking for the right words, "-something else."

Jeff shook his head and snorted. "Nice try, sunshine, but I don't believe you."

Sandra was shaking next to him. Her face was devoid of all colour and her lips were a stretched line. "What do you want?"

"What I want, your tiny little minds wouldn't be able to comprehend."

"You've gone mental pal." James said, in his best Scottish accent. "You expect us to believe we're talking to – what? The Devil? Because a fire went out!" He started to laugh.

Mark felt a smile return to his face, some of James' bravado rubbing off on him. He would be able to patch things up with Elana and forget this nasty, horrible man had ever spoken to him. This was all some stupid practical joke that was going badly wrong. But even then, Mark knew that wasn't entirely true. Something deep down was telling him to run. Run hard and fast, and not stop.

"How did he know about-" Bruce started.

"Don't," Elana said. "He's just a sick pathetic man. I don't know how he knew, but there will be a reason." She focussed her attention on Mark. "Please forgive me. It was years ago and nothing to do with how great we are now."

Before Mark could say anything, Adam leapt to his feet, making them all recoil slightly. Even James jumped at the sudden movement. He moved closer to the group, smiling all the time.

"You need some convincing?" he said. "Well, let's try this. Jeff, you think Sandra's been having an affair with Simon from the walking group."

"What?" Jeff said, looking round the group for moral support.

"I'm doing no such thing!" Sandra shouted.

"No, but his wife is a different thing altogether now isn't it?"

Mark hadn't thought it possible, but Sandra turned even paler.

"You've been walking with her for about six months now haven't you? At first there was a whole group of you, but then you and her started to go for other walks, just the two of you." Adam's smile widened. "At first, you were flattered: she's younger than you isn't she? Tracey, right?"

Sandra found herself nodding. Jeff couldn't take his eyes from his wife, his slack jawed expression telling everyone that he hadn't suspected anything like this.

"Her firm body would brush past yours on narrow paths. Again, to begin with, you didn't think anything of it did you? But you started to like it, the attention starved glamorous wife and the young, gorgeous woman out on walks. You started to fantasise about what it would be like, so when she made that move you gladly accepted."

"Shut up," Sandra said. She was trying to avoid Jeff's gaze, but her eye kept flitting to his. The hurt on his face was apparent for all to see.

"It's not true," he said hoarsely.

"She kissed you out at Clovelly Dykes. Her lips felt so soft, no stubble, and when her tongue touched yours, oh, how it set you on fire." Adam started rubbing himself with one hand and moaning. The other hand remained behind his back. "She slipped her hand in your wet knickers and wanked you into a frenzy didn't she? You haven't come like that in years – certainly not with Jeff."

"You, you *bitch*," Jeff cried.

Mark frowned. *Something's wrong. Why is his hand behind his back?*

"But you had guilt didn't you? You grabbed her firm tits, but then remembered your pathetic husband and got cold feet. You didn't even have the decency to throw a few fingers into her. She makes you come like that and you leave her wanting more. Quite clever really. Always leave them wanting more."

"You bastard!" Jeff roared and he rushed at Adam.

"Jeff, no!" Sandra screamed.

James, Mark and Bruce leapt to their feet, ready to help Jeff. *Where's the axe?* The thought came too late. Far too late. Mark heard a swishing noise and realised what had happened a fraction too late. Adam had picked up Bruce's axe when he stood up. No-one had seen him do it, but he swung it now.

The axe blade cut into Jeff's neck, sinking deep enough to sever his artery. Blood sprayed out of the wound, splashing the fireplace and the tables with thick blood. The metallic smell of iron filed the room at the same time that Sandra's screams deafened them all. Jeff gurgled blood out of his mouth and sank to his knees. Adam pulled the axe free, and blood shot across the room, splattering the wall above the fireplace.

The three men stopped in their tracks, five feet from Adam. Jeff toppled over and lay in a crumpled heap, blood spreading around his head. Adam, also covered in blood, grinned at the three, and rested the axe on his shoulder like he was taking a break from chopping wood.

"I wouldn't," he said.

They didn't.

Chapter 12

Eventually, Sandra's screams gave way to sobs that made her whole body convulse. She remained deathly pale, except for her red rimmed puffy eyes. Black lines of running mascara made train tracks down her face to her shaking shoulders. Elana was holding her as tight as a vice, but was powerless to stop the trembling.

Mark was speechless. Events had never overtaken him to such a degree before; he had never felt so helpless or out of control. They were being held hostage by a madman with an axe who seemed delusional with it. In addition, he seemed to have knowledge of individuals in the group that indicated he'd done some research into them. He didn't want to consider the implications of that. He also didn't want to think about what Adam would come out with next, or who would face the axe. *We have to get out of here.*

Adam sat beside the fire, axe resting casually against his leg, eyes flitting from one person to the next, never settling for long. It was as if he were doing some kind of playground counting; all that was missing was the 'eeny, meeny, miny, moe'.

"Get me a drink," he said, pointing at James.

"I've never pulled a pint in my life," James said. His eyes and nose were still swollen but the blood around his mouth had dried. He was sitting next to Mark, a show of solidarity in the face of the maniac.

"Well, it would be a shame for your life to end without you trying now, wouldn't it?"

"Just pull it towards you and tilt the glass. It really is as easy as it looks," Bruce said and looked at Adam briefly before continuing, "Glasses are on the shelf under the bar."

James got to his feet and stepped over Jeff's corpse to get to the bar. He made a point of scanning the shelves, hoping that his eyes hadn't rested on what lay on the shelf underneath the till and he picked up a glass.

"What do you want?" he asked.

"World peace," Adam said and laughed. No-one joined in. Elana kept her arm around Sandra and was now whispering soothing words in her ears. Bruce and Saran were hugging each other next to them. Bruce kept looking between James and Adam and a thin sheen of sweat adorned his brow.

"You're sick," James said.

"That's because Brucie here has no idea how to keep beer. The morning after, well, what a smell." Adam laughed again, but then stopped. "Tough crowd, huh?"

James moved quickly. He pulled the gun from under the bar and aimed it straight at Adam. The stock was tight against his shoulder so he was ashamed to see the end of the barrel tremble. He aimed it at the middle of Adam's chest.

Everybody stood up at the same time.

"Shoot!" Mark yelled.

"You don't have the nerve," Adam said. "Well, do you, pretty boy?" He appeared to be the only calm person in the room. James squeezed the trigger, just like they said to in countless films he'd seen. The shotgun bucked in his hands, crashing into his shoulder with the force of a sledge-hammer. He heard a crack, and searing white hot pain shot down the right hand side of his body.

Adam took the shot in the middle of the chest. He fell back against a table and rolled to the floor, face down. From outside the pub they heard a high pitched whining sound.

"Yes!" Mark shouted.

"What the fuck is that?" James asked. Beads of sweat had formed on his forehead and he was holding his left arm at a strange angle, but he hadn't let go of the shotgun.

They turned towards the door as it buckled on its hinges. Mark thought of the bolt holding the door in place. *We don't have long.*

"The monks!" Elana cried.

The door banged again.

"Run!" Bruce shouted. "Upstairs, quickly!"

Saran led the way, dragging Sandra by the hand. Elana ran to Mark and hugged him. He didn't hug back, but kept his eyes on the fallen

Adam. James aimed the shotgun at the door, smoke curling from one of the barrels.

"Come on!" Elana pleaded, pulling at Mark's arm. He ignored her.

"Fellas, we should go," Bruce said, holding the door open.

Adam sat up. "Son of a bitch!" he roared.

Elana screamed. Mark stepped forward and kicked hard. His boot caught Adam under the chin forcing his head back, thudding onto the stone floor with a sickening thump. Mark grabbed Elana's wrist, far too firmly for comfort.

"Let's go."

They reached the door when a shout came from behind them. James was still aiming the gun at the door, but the moaning came from the floor. Adam got to his knees, spat blood onto the floor then stood up slowly. His shirt had a hole in the middle of his chest and blood oozed out of the wound it revealed.

He pointed at James and let out a roar. The noise made Elana's knees tremble and she felt a growing pit of nausea in her stomach. The wound in Adam's chest looked so raw, he shouldn't be breathing, let alone standing. For the first time, she began to doubt her knowledge of the world.

"Holy shit," James said and pulled the trigger of the shotgun. The side of Adam's face exploded in a shower of red and white shards of bone that flew away from his head. The blood and bone fragments decorated the walls and carpet. Adam fell to the floor once more.

"Yes!" James shouted.

The door to the pub flew off its hinges, banging into the nearest table with a crash that shook the windows. Standing in the doorway were several of the monks and they charged into the room, all making the horrible screeching noise they had heard when Adam had first been shot.

Mark pulled Elana after him as he ran down the short corridor. James ran behind him, but stopped at the bottom of the stairs. Mark looked back at him and was surprised to see him grinning.

"Go! I'll hold them off!" James said. He looked back down the corridor, gun raised. His shoulder looked wrong: it hung lower than his other shoulder and his arm hung limply by his side. He was managing to hold the gun up, but only just.

"Come on!" Mark shouted.

"Take her and go!" James shouted again.

Elana started to push Mark up the stairs. "Come on!"

They reached the landing and looked back down, but James wasn't focussing on them, he was looking down the short corridor.

"What's going to happen to him?" Elana asked, her voice breaking.

"He'll be fine," Mark said, all the while knowing that he wouldn't be. They heard a shout from the end room of the corridor and saw Bruce gesturing at them to hurry up. They dashed to the room, and Mark took Bruce's place at the door. He looked down the corridor, waiting, hoping for a sign of his old friend.

James felt his insides turn cold as the first monk came into view. His body was racked with pain, from his broken nose down to whatever he had done to his shoulder. Despite the pain, he had never felt so alive – it was as if he had a reason to live now: fighting for his life.

"Stop! I have a gun!" he roared. In his mind, he had images of Clint Eastwood at the end of *Unforgiven*, shouting at Gene Hackman's men and bluffing them into submission.

The monk stopped but said nothing. Instead he raised his arm but the folds of his robe hid his hand from view.

"Fuck you," James roared and pulled the trigger.

The gun clicked empty.

The monk laughed, his whole habit shaking. Suddenly, James was deafened by a loud bang. Something hit him in the stomach and it took James a second to realise he'd been shot. White hot pain lanced through his body and he stumbled back against the stairs with a grunt.

More of the monks came round the corner, but they were silent now. They stood around the doorway, all still, like they were waiting for something. *This is it, this is the moment. I'm going to die at the hands of some weird monks of Satan.* He started to shake, both adrenaline and fear racking his nervous system. Bile rose in his throat and he tried to force it down, but to no avail. He vomited on the stairs and could barely lift his head out of the mess when he was done. This was not quite the glorious end he had envisaged. It was always so much more glamorous in the films.

"Hello, James."

He looked up at the words, couldn't comprehend what he was seeing and then started to scream.

The screams were unlike anything Mark had ever heard. He had once spent a day in casualty with a broken wrist when a man had come in with a broken arm of his own. This man's bone was sticking through his shirt and blood was pouring out of the wound. The screams coming from that man were nothing like this. That noise had been the grunts and groans of a man in pain. This noise consisted of a combination of abject terror and pain that no one should have to endure. When the screams abruptly stopped, he knew that James was gone.

He closed the door quietly, tears rolling down his face. All his anger at James was gone. He would never be able to apologise for the attack, for breaking his nose, for somehow thinking that his friend had tried to steal his girlfriend. Mark slid down the door, sitting with his back to it, knees up and he started to sob.

"What's happened?" shrieked Sandra. She was really starting to get on Mark's nerves.

"James," Elana said just above a whisper. "They've killed James."

"Who has? What do you mean, killed him?"

Saran slapped her, once. Sandra held her hand to her bright red cheek and started to cry. "Pull yourself together," Saran snapped. "You're going to let them know where we are."

"It's not going to take them long to figure it out is it?" Bruce muttered.

"We need to leave," Elana pleaded. "We need to get out of here."

"Look at the weather!" Bruce said. "We go out in that, and we'll all die before we get a mile down the road."

"We stay here and we die anyway," Elana said.

"We could fight back," Saran said.

"With what? We've got no weapons."

"There are knives in the kitchen."

"A knife against an axe? Don't be stupid," Elana said.

"We can get the gun," Saran said. "James had the shotgun."

"James is dead. They have the gun now," Mark said, lifting his head from his knees. "We're all going to die."

Chapter 13

Silence followed Mark's declaration. He remained sat on the floor with his head on his knees. Tears rolled down his cheeks and silent sobs racked his body.

Elana felt sick to the pit of her stomach, but she forced herself to go to him and she put her arm around his shoulders. She pulled him to her and he buried his head in the pit of her shoulder and neck.

"I'm so sorry," she whispered.

He said nothing but his sobs subsided slightly.

"Please forgive me."

He remained silent.

"I don't want to die with you hating me."

That got his attention. He gazed into her eyes as if looking for the truth. "I don't hate you."

Now she felt tears well in her own eyes. Relief flooded through her; they would get through this.

"I will never be able to tell James that I forgive *him*," Mark said. "That he has nothing to be forgiven for."

"I'm so sorry," she said again.

"Stop saying that. What's done is done. It was years ago." *And how you laughed at the story. James' description of this lovely young bint sucking him off in a night club. He'd then ditched the bint, gone to a different club and pulled someone else. That one he took back to where there were staying. Typical James.*

Bruce sat down next to them. His face was pale but he appeared calm. Only a wild look in his eyes betrayed his terror.

"We need to get out of here," Bruce said. "We need a plan."

"Make one then," Mark said.

Elana patted his shoulder. "Come on, hon, we need you."

"What can I do? There's so many of them."

"Do we actually know for sure how many there are?" Elana said.

95

"There were twelve outside in the snow. If they've all come in, then-" Bruce didn't finish the sentence; he didn't need to.

"What if we talk to them?" Saran said. She was whispering but it was still loud enough for them to hear it clearly across the room. Bruce winced and beckoned her over. She took Sandra's hand and came over to the door and they sat in a rough semicircle around Mark and Elana. Mark kept his back firmly against the door.

"They killed Jeff and James," Mark said. "Somehow I don't think that having a chat is high on their agenda." His frown returned. *Bruce is right. We need a plan.*

"James is dead?" Sandra asked. No-one answered.

Mark took in the surroundings for the first time. It was a different room to the one he and Elana had been in earlier. *Not even two hours ago.* How different things had been then. Basking in the afterglow of sex, the world had seemed a far saner place. The room shared similar furnishings to the other one: A solitary wardrobe; a solid looking chest of drawers and an ottoman at the foot of the bed. *Hope there's no dummy in that one.* A large window sat in the middle of the opposite wall. He could see that snow lined the window sill and condensation had fogged up the inside.

He couldn't see enough to tell if the snow was still falling, but it was clear that outside was not an option: snow would slow them down and maybe it was cold enough to cause a real problem.

"We need to get help," Elana said.

"How?" Bruce asked. "Mobiles don't work here, unless we get to the top of the hill by the cairn. The landline is downstairs and the radio is in the generator building."

"Wi-Fi? I can use that to make a call," Elana said.

Bruce shook his head. "Walls are too thick. I've ordered one of those booster things, but it's not arrived yet."

"You need to stand next to the router to get a Wi-Fi signal here," Saran said.

"We're too far away from Princetown to get any kind of meaningful speed. I doubt it would support voice calling."

"Ok then, how far away is the cairn?" Elana asked.

"Not far, maybe a hundred metres or so," Saran answered. "It's all uphill and it's wild moorland."

"So?"

"So there's holes, pits and ditches to fall into, all of which have probably been covered by drifting snow."

"Where's the phone?" Elana persisted. She was not prepared to roll over and just give up.

"It's in the kitchen."

Mark looked at Bruce. "We can get to the kitchen. It's separate to the bar."

He nodded. "Yes, unless they're in the kitchen too."

"Well, in that case we create a diversion," Elana said. "Make them think we're escaping or something."

"I've got a better idea," Mark said, getting to his feet. "I'm going to go talk to them. That'll be enough of a diversion."

"That's the most stupid thing I've heard today," Bruce said. "You just said talking wasn't high on their agenda."

"Well, you've got someone downstairs who just told us he's the devil, so I don't think it's that stupid."

"You can't," Elana said, pulling him towards her again.

"There is no better idea," Mark said. "Look, I go downstairs and talk to them, Bruce sneaks into the kitchen and rings the police. We barricade ourselves in here till the cavalry arrive." He shrugged. "Simple."

"They won't talk to you!" Elana cried.

"They might," Mark said. "Look, their ring leader is dead, James shot him, twice I think. Whatever their plan was, it's changed. Maybe they'll listen to common sense. None of us could identify them so maybe they can disappear before the police get here."

They all considered his words. Sandra resumed crying, the noise breaking the silence.

"You know I'm right," Mark said. "This is our only chance."

"It doesn't have to be you," Elana said. "Someone else could go talk to them."

He shook his head. "I can't ask someone else to do this, I wouldn't be able to live with myself."

"They'll kill you!" Elana cried.

"Maybe," he said like it was the most obvious thing in the world. "But I don't think so. Whatever mad plan they had, it's changed, okay?"

"Let him go!" Sandra said. Elana shot her a look that almost brought the words 'if looks could kill' to life.

"There must be another way."

97

"Look outside. That's not an option. We stay in this room, eventually we die. This way, help gets to be on the way and you can barricade yourself in."

Saran nodded. She didn't look happy at the thought of Bruce going to make the phone call, but she could see the sense of Mark's words.

"What's your plan?" Bruce asked, his voice quiet.

"I go down stairs, basically talk to them."

"This is a shit plan, Mark," Bruce said.

"Yeah, I know, but-" he paused, forcing himself to smile at Bruce. "When I've got their attention, you get to the phone, radio, whatever."

"Wait," Elana said. "Is there a computer in the building? We could send emails to the police or something."

"Computer's downstairs," Saran said. "It's in the office."

"Where's that?"

"Next to the kitchen."

"Office is a grand word for it. It's an old broom cupboard basically, it might even have been a larder once upon a time," Bruce said.

"Try the phone first," Mark said. "Do you leave your computer on?"

Bruce nodded.

"Good." He took a deep breath. "Ramblers, let's get rambling."

"Mark-" Elana said but stopped. "Love you." She kissed him on the mouth and then he and Bruce were gone, closing the door quietly behind them. Her hand drifted to her belly. *Why didn't I tell him?* She resolved to tell him when she saw him again.

She tried not to think that, maybe, just maybe, she wouldn't.

Mark crept along the corridor, back firmly pressed to the wall. Bruce followed a couple of feet behind. Neither made a sound and the thick carpet meant that their footsteps didn't give them away. He peered over the top of the stairs and saw two of the monks at the bottom of the stairs. They had their backs to him. He shrank back instantly, holding up his hand for Bruce to stop. He held up two fingers and Bruce nodded. Mark stepped to the middle of the corridor and held his hands up as he started down the stairs.

"Hey!" He walked slowly down the stairs, each step deliberate and his feet took forever to reach the next step down. "I'm not armed. I want to talk to you."

The monks turned as slowly as he walked. Their faces remained hidden in the dark cowls of their hoods. The black ovals raised to look at him and he had to stop. The knot of anxiety in his stomach grew. *This is a huge mistake.* The stench of vomit was overpowering.

Behind the monks, he could see a long trail of red gore that looked like it had been painted onto the carpet. *James.* The knot grew exponentially. The trail ended by the door that went back into the bar. To the left was the open doorway that led through to the kitchen. If any monks were in there, then they were sunk before they had even started.

"I want to talk to you," Mark said. "Just talk, okay?" He hoped his voice didn't give away how nervous he felt. The monks remained silent. "Who's in charge?" He had nearly said 'take me to your leader' and a strange half laugh barked out of his mouth. He realised that sweat was forming on his brow.

The door to the pub opened and a voice said, "Bring him to me."

Mark thought he recognised the voice, but that wasn't possible. Before he could think more about that, the two monks ran forward and started to hit him around the head. He fell to the floor, rolling down the last few steps as the blows rained down on him. *Come on Bruce. It's up to you now.*

It was the bravest thing Bruce had ever witnessed first-hand. Of course he had read books about soldiers in war doing crazy things to rescue fallen comrades or putting themselves in danger so the unit could escape. As a younger man he had been fascinated with the story of Dunkirk and specifically the soldiers who were ordered to slow the German advance so the British could get to the beach. Many of those had died so others could live and he had often tried to think about what those men must have thought as they watched their friends go to the beaches and, ultimately, safety.

Now, as he watched Mark, he had an idea of what those men had been through. It was survival, pure and simple: live through each moment and then worry about what the next one brings. He watched from the top of the stairs as the monks battered Mark. Bruce thought about joining the fight, helping Mark out, but that wasn't the plan.

He had a job to do.

Nevertheless, he felt sick as the monks hit Mark to the floor and then hit him some more for good measure. They dragged him and used his head to push the door to the bar open. He had heard the voice and like Mark, couldn't believe it.

Focus! He crept down the stairs, holding his breath all the way. The thick carpet, which had seemed such an extravagance when they first moved in, was proving a godsend. He gagged at the smell of vomit. At the bottom of the stairs, he crouched over, keeping his back to the wall. This was partly to keep himself hidden from view but mostly to stop from standing in the trail of blood that snaked towards the door to the bar. He tried not to think about the fact that it was James' remains he was avoiding.

The door to the kitchen had been propped open with a wedge of wood. He went through the door then quietly removed the door stop. Holding the door handle to prevent the door from slamming, he held his breath at the deafening click it made as it shut. He stood stock still, clutching the handle, still in the half crouch he had used to walk along the corridor, eyes wide. In other circumstances, he would have felt very foolish.

Nobody came.

He dared to breathe again and looked around the kitchen. It seemed so normal, like nothing had changed. The last time he had stood in here, he had been talking to Saran about the lack of wood for the fire. Seemed trivial now. If all they had to worry about was chopping wood for a fire, then the world would seem right again.

He had put the corded phone on the wall a week ago so that it could be easily reached from the office or kitchen. Another phone was due to be installed in the bar, but the engineer had been booked all over Christmas and so it was going to be done next week instead. *A good thing really, I don't want anyone in the bar to know I'm on the phone.* He put a wireless handset at the top of his next shopping list.

Bruce picked up the handset and held it to his ear. No dial tone. He hit the receiver button several times, but still no tone. He swore to himself and put the handset back down. Maybe the storm had brought the wires down. Maybe the monks had cut the lines. Either way, no phone call was being made tonight.

He stepped into the office, already thinking that this would be a waste of time. The computer's screensaver glowed at him. A swirling banner read "You should be working!" as it zoomed around the screen. He flicked the mouse and the familiar pattern of icons came into view. The background picture was of Saran and him on the Greek island of Alonissos. That had been the holiday they had decided to sell up and buy a pub. The hopes and excitement of that decision came back to him on seeing the photograph - but it was looking like such a bad idea now.

He clicked on the Firefox icon and waited for the familiar homepage to appear. The circle next to his mouse pointer swam round and round for an age until the 'Page 404' error came up telling him to check he was connected to the internet.

Bruce swore inwardly again.

No phones. No internet.

Now what?

The kitchen door creaked open.

Chapter 14

Mark opened his eyes, blinked a few times and waited for the room to come into focus. His left eye felt strange; it was swollen to the point of being closed. He had a ringing in his ears and his lips felt twice their normal size. All in all, he knew he had been given a good kicking.

"Hello again, Mark."

Mark lifted his head and recoiled, trying to get away from the figure in front of him. His legs pushed on the carpet, making his chair tip backwards. He tried to put his hands out to stop the fall and only then realised he was tied to the chair. A firm hand pushed in the middle of his back and he was upright again. He started to turn his head to see who was behind him and earned a punch for his troubles. His chin felt wet suddenly and he knew his lips were bleeding.

"Mark, I said you were a leader," Adam said, his voice dripping with sarcasm. He sat a few feet away from Mark, facing him. Behind Adam stood two of the monks, and Mark guessed there were probably another two behind his chair. Nobody else was in the room, but he couldn't think about that – his attention was focussed on Adam only. He wanted to look away; wanted to run screaming into the night actually.

Adam had a hole in his chest where the shotgun blast had hit him. Blood pulsed out of it rhythmically with every heartbeat. Dried blood caked the wound with a thick black crust and bits of bone could be seen through the hole. Despite this, it was the face that Mark couldn't drag his gaze from. The second shot had hit Adam in the head; he had seen that with his own eyes. The right side of Adam's face was ruined; the skin dissolved into a red mess that used to be his cheek; His eye socket was empty, with the flesh around it a curious mix of red, orange and black. The centre of the socket was black. The top of his head was scorched, with hair missing on only one side, as if he had been burnt. Adam grinned at him, white teeth incongruous in the ruined face.

"What's the matter, Mark, are you not pleased to see me?"

Mark swallowed bile and started to hyperventilate. He took deep breaths and tried to calm himself down. He was trembling all over, and his bladder emptied, the sudden warmth making him curiously embarrassed.

"You should be dead."

"Yes."

Adam gave him a moment to process this information.

"Oh God, oh God, oh God."

Adam chuckled. "Weird isn't it? You've spent your whole life denying Him, but the moment the shit hits the fan, there you are squawking for Him. Pathetic really, I expected more from you, Mark."

"This is impossible."

"No. Believe your eyes. I tried to tell you all what was happening, but you wouldn't listen."

"You're not the Devil," Mark said. "You can't be."

"I am what I am."

"What do you want?"

"My motives are my own. I wouldn't expect you to understand."

"You can't be the Devil," Mark said again. His breathing had calmed down and he was feeling more in control. Logic and common sense were beginning to make inroads into his fear.

"Why not?"

"If I'm not a Christian, you have no power over me."

"Don't be so naïve. I have many names from many places. Mara, Asura, the adversary, Iblis, the hinderer; even those crazy Zoroastrians have a name for me: Ahriman. It's the physical body of Angra Mainyu. I like that one, has a certain ring to it."

"You're nuts," Mark said. Adam just stared at him. The silence stretched to breaking point before Mark spoke again. "A well-read nut, but nuts all the same."

"That's more like it Mark, get a bit of humour in there."

"Why are you doing this?"

"I told you once. Pay attention, Mark. My motives are far too complex for your tiny little brain to comprehend."

"If you're going to kill us, why not just get on with it?"

"I have my reasons."

"You've already killed two of my friends."

"Friends?" Adam chuckled. "You only met Jeff tonight. He was a pain in the arse, you thought that."

"I didn't," Mark said.

"Please Mark, this will go so much better for you if you tell me the truth. I already know anyway."

Mark said nothing, his mind wouldn't settle on any single thought. Despite this, he felt a strange calm, almost accepting of the situation. There was no way he was talking to the devil, he just had to keep the guy calm until help arrived. *Easy, feed his ego, let him think that everyone is quaking in their boots.* At least part of that would not be difficult.

"So, you thought Jeff was a dick and James," Adam scoffed, "well, where do we start with him?"

"James was a good man."

Adam laughed out loud, causing fresh blood to pulse out of the wound in his chest. The laugh distorted the ruined face further and Mark wondered if plastic surgery was available in prisons. *Jesus, Mark, focus.*

"James was a complete bastard and you know it. It's why he died: I love a bastard, me."

"He-"

"Save it, Mark." Adam rolled his good eye, like a teacher showing disappointment in a good student who has underperformed. "In addition to coming all over your girlfriend's face, he has stolen money, used people and doesn't care about anyone other than himself."

"She wasn't my girlfriend." Mark tried to stop the anger rising in him.

"Well, technically no, but how do you feel about wanting to marry such a slut?"

Mark forced himself to laugh. "Try harder man. If I judged or refused to be with anyone with baggage or who had done something stupid when they were younger, I'd be on my own forever. Hell, I'd have to kill myself."

"Now you're getting it."

Mark stopped. He had been building up to a great speech about the fragility of humans, but the quietness of Adam's words made him sick to the stomach.

"James died saving us," Mark said. "He wasn't the man you thought he was."

"No, Mark," Adam shook his head and he looked genuinely sad for a second. The look was just wrong on the bloody face. "He wasn't the man *you* thought he was."

"He-"

"-treated women like they were second class citizens. Now don't get me wrong Mark, I'm all for that. In fact, you could say that's what I'm all about." Adam turned to the monk on his left and laughed. The monk's cowl shook, but no sound came from it. "In fact, he treated everyone badly, always taking, taking, taking."

"He was a teacher. He spent his life educating people."

Adam laughed again. "No, Mark. Do you know anything about teachers? Some of them, yes, they are in it for the noble side of it: educating, helping people to help themselves. Teach a man to fish and all that. Sickening really. Most of them are in it for the pay and the holidays. But some of them are in it to be close to those burgeoning teenage girls and boys. All that sexual tension in a room, mmm, mmm." Adam licked his lips and Mark cringed. "Maybe next time I'll be a teacher. I'll let you decide which type James was."

"So, if you're Lucifer, where is your host?" Mark tried to change the subject. *James didn't like young girls whatever this bastard thinks. He's wrong.*

"I never said I was Lucifer." Adam looked genuinely surprised. "Have you been paying attention?"

"You said you were the Devil. That's Lucifer."

"You have such a narrow view of the world Mark."

"Inferior to God, that's what the Catholics said." Mark racked his brains, wishing he had paid more attention in RE lessons at school. It was all too long ago.

"Catholics? What do they know? Fretting about guilt the whole time. Who gave them that idea?" Adam's horrible smile was back. "Just who do you think makes them feel guilty all the time?"

"Ah, come on," Mark said. "You really expect me to believe that you are some all-powerful deity who influences people?"

"Deity?" Adam said. "Good word. Did you remember that from your sad Dungeons and Dragons days?"

"So, you're the one who makes priests do nasty things to little boys? Cause's wars? Creates murderers? Induces famine?" Mark said. "Yet you choose to come to a little pub in Devon? You're nuts."

"Never underestimate the fucked up mess that humans are more than willing to force upon themselves. I've never once made someone

105

start a war. Osama Bin Laden was nothing to do with me, nor Hitler, Genghis Khan or all those wonderful serial killers. Paedophiles, the bogeymen of today, corrupting so much innocence. They're too easy. I didn't even give them a nudge. No, you'll see me in the petty everyday things. Shout at someone because they cut you up in your car? Swear at the person who didn't hold a door for you? Those, now those, I love. Good people doing bad things, having nasty thoughts. I can't get enough of it. See, everyone *expects* me in the bad, but I'm there in the good too. I'm all the petty, horrible little things you do every single day of your life."

Mark sat in silence, mulling over the words. In reality he was trying to think of a way out of the situation. *What can we do? The man was insane. The way he is bleeding he will surely die soon. Actually, why the hell isn't he dead already?* Mark had no clue as to how long it would take someone to bleed out, six hours maybe? How long had he been unconscious? Probably a couple of minutes, maybe half an hour. So, at most, it had been an hour since Adam had been shot. If Bruce had made the call, it would be up to another hour before anyone came to help – maybe longer as the snow was still bad. In short it didn't look good: Adam had killed two people within ten minutes; at that rate he would kill them all within the next hour. They had to escape, get away – but how?

"What do you want from us?" Mark asked again.

"Give it a rest Mark, I'm not explaining this. I can't – as you say – be arsed." Adam leant closer. "Let's just say I'm here to have some fun – that, you can understand." He winked his good eye; the other remained open and dark. Mark tore his gaze away. "Just like you and Elana."

"So your fun is killing people? Just kill me then, get it over with."

"No, no, no, Mark. I've no interest in killing you. That gets me nothing. You could walk out of here tonight if you play your cards right." Adam seemed to remember something and laughed. "Of course, I've taken a card player from here before. He tried to trick me you know. He won't make that mistake again."

Mark had no idea what Adam was talking about. "Answer the question."

"I'm not here to kill you Mark. That gains me nothing."

"So let us go then."

Adam laughed. "No, not just yet."

"What do you want?"

106

"I want your love." Adam stood quickly, arms spread like Christ on the cross. Fresh blood coursed out of his wounds. "I want you to worship me."

"Ok, I love you." Mark said, looking up at the bloodied figure. "Now let us all go."

"No, no, no," Adam said. "By the end of the night you will worship me. Mark my words, Mark," he grinned at his monks again, "by the end of the night if you want to live you will give me your undisputed, undivided, unequivocal love."

Bruce held his breath and ducked behind the island. He heard the door creak shut and a footstep into the room. Sitting with his back to the counter, he was opposite the computer room. The kitchen wasn't very big, so if he moved, he would be discovered. He looked left and right, seeing cupboards and the ridiculously large fridge freezer, but nothing useful like a weapon. The cooker and hob were to his right and slightly behind him. They both ran on gas – could he turn it on and set fire to the monk? No, stupid idea; he wasn't an action hero and he would probably end up burning the whole pub down.

He looked left again. The cupboards on the wall in front of him stopped by the back entrance. A corkboard sat on the wall, waiting for information to be posted on it. Above him, the order rack ran in an oval and he wondered if it would ever have a ticket on it again. He tried to picture the top of the counter: was it where the knives were kept? The kitchen was Saran's place – she had practically banned him after the second time he had piled all the dishes in the wrong cupboard.

He heard breathing. Deep, deliberate, slow breathing that turned his blood cold. *Think! Where are the knives?* He heard the footsteps again, a steady thump on the tiled floor: the monk was going to the right. There was nothing for it, he would have to move or else be discovered. Bruce crawled to the left on all fours. He expected to hear a shout at any moment, but none came. He risked a quick look round the edge of the counter, but all he could see was the door. He scurried around and drew his arms and legs into his body so that no part of him could be seen from the other side of the kitchen.

The breathing sounded so close it was as if it were in his ear. It was almost like the monk wanted him to know he was there. He wanted to look, needed to check the monk's position. What if he just ran? How far could he get? The door to the garden was next to the computer cupboard – why hadn't he ducked outside when he had the chance?

Because it's freezing out there. He would die quickly, especially as he only had a shirt on the top half of his body. *Going to die in here if the monk finds you.* The heavy breathing stopped.

As he became more anxious, Bruce felt pain across his chest, rising up the left hand side. His heart felt as if someone had it in a vice. *Oh Christ, I'm going to have a heart attack.* Blood thundered in his ears and he felt bile rise up his throat. *Don't be sick!* He swallowed, shuddering at the taste of the bile. The pain in his chest subsided slowly and he began to feel more normal. His body was letting him down and he didn't know whether the monk, the cold or his heart would get him first. He needed to know where the monk was.

He peered around the edge of the counter.

Mark shook his head, panic rising in his throat. There was something about the way Adam had said the words; Mark had never had a religious experience, never been in the slightest bit interested in religion, but he felt the power of Adam's words; the conviction in his voice was clear. Whatever the truth of the situation, Adam believed what he was saying and that made him a very dangerous man.

"You'll be dead by morning," Mark said. "Look at the state of you."

Adam waved his hand in a dismissive gesture. "Just a flesh wound." That horrible laugh. "Go back to the others Mark. Go and convince them to give me their love."

"And if I refuse?" Mark said.

A genuine look of confusion crossed Adam's face. "Why would you refuse?"

"Because you're crazy and you're going to die." Mark felt exasperation. The man was stupid and mad.

"You let me worry about these wounds, Mark. Believe me, they are not as bad as they look, though they do smart a little." Adam laughed again and the monks shook along with him.

"You could let us help you. We could call an ambulance, they'll save you."

"Call them how? The phones are dead. Mobile phones don't work here. The radio in the shed has been smashed. Just how do you plan on contacting anyone?"

Mark felt a stab of fear for Bruce. The plan was not going to work if Bruce couldn't raise help. Would he be able to get back upstairs without being discovered?

"You need to face facts Mark. Look at what's going on. Two are already dead. No-one else needs to die tonight."

"Without an ambulance you will die." Mark could feel sweat trickling down his forehead.

"You still refuse to believe who I am. I cannot die."

"Three hours ago, you were an obnoxious bar fly with shit under his fingers, now you're the Prince of Darkness?" Mark snorted. "Whatever you've been smoking, I want some."

Adam leapt to his feet and pressed his face close to Mark's, a snarl on his lips. Mark shrank back in the chair, but the ties didn't let him get far. "You need to open your eyes. The world is far more complex than you imagine."

Mark took a deep breath and set his jaw. He put his face back towards Adam, until their noses were almost touching. The empty socket and blood turned his stomach, but he held his position, trying not to let his revulsion show.

"I believe in good and evil. I believe that everyone has the capacity for both. Even the most rampant serial killer might have a soft spot for a puppy. Hitler loved Eva Braun. Saddam just wanted the best for his people, his family. None of them were influenced by you. If I swear at someone because they cut me up or spill my beer, that's not you, that's me - my failings as a human. It doesn't make me a bad person. I don't believe in God or angels or any of that Sunday school shit-"

Adam was laughing, making Mark stop his rant.

"What the fuck?" Mark shouted, anger straining his voice.

"Did you hear?" Adam drew himself back from Mark and looked at the monks. They were shaking again. "Did you hear what he said?"

"What? What the fuck did I say?"

"You," Adam said simply. "You said: 'If I swear at someone because they cut me up or spill my beer, that's not you.'"

He laughed again, head back, mouth open wide and whole body wracked with the convulsion of the laugh.

"You're starting to believe, Mark."

Bruce came face to feet with the monk. He screamed and jumped up, catching the monk with the back of his head as he rose. The reverse head butt pushed the monk back, with a satisfying crunch. Pain lanced through Bruce's head, but he ignored it; he had to get the next blow in, keep the monk on his back foot. The monk was still off balance from the blow so Bruce kicked as hard as he could between the man's legs. All the air rushed out of the man's lungs as he doubled over in agony. Bruce then brought his knee up into the man's face.

Years before, Bruce had known some people from a very rough part of the valleys in Wales. They had taught him the technique: balls, chin, leg it. The first two parts had worked extremely well, better than expected. The monk had fallen back to the counter, doubled over and holding on to the counter with one hand whilst his free hand went to his face. A low moan came from deep within the cowl. He sank to the floor.

Time for part three of the technique: Bruce ran.

He brushed past the monk, heading for the back door. He just wanted to get out, get away from the pub. He was less than five feet from the door when he felt his legs give way. He fell to the floor with a surprised yelp, only just getting his hands underneath him to break his fall. Bruce tried to push himself back to his feet, but slipped and couldn't move his left leg.

The monk had hold of his foot.

Bruce drove his free foot down, smashing onto the monk's hand with all his might. He was aware that he was screaming and that the monk was moaning. Too noisy – someone would hear and come. Panic rose within him again, and Bruce kicked down harder still. Using reserves of strength he didn't know he had, he pushed his foot down with all the force he could muster. He heard bones crunch beneath his foot, but still the monk didn't let go. Bruce forced himself up, hopping onto his right leg and grabbed hold of the counter top. Something caught his eye on the counter.

The knives.

They were just out of reach. His fingertips brushed them and he almost burst into tears. The monk's grip changed on his leg, pulling on his trousers. Bruce didn't need to look down to know the monk was climbing up his leg, using the jeans to pull himself to his feet.

"NO!" Bruce screamed. His fingers closed round the handle of a knife and he brought it round in a sweeping arc, stabbing down where the monk was. The blade made a scratching noise as it cut into the monk.

Bruce brought it back up and stabbed down again and again. At some point the monk let go of his leg and Bruce pounced, not once stopping the movement of the blade. The monk's moan turned to a gurgle and his legs began to spasm. Blood was pouring from the hood, staining the monk's robe an even deeper brown. The floor was rapidly turning from pristine white to crimson red.

Bruce continued to stab and scream until all other sounds in the kitchen stopped and the twitching had ceased. He was covered in blood and sweat. His heart rate was through the roof. He looked down at the monk who was - clearly - dead. The hood had fallen back now revealing the ruined face, surrounded by a mass of blonde hair that was turning as red as the floor.

Bruce was looking at the corpse of a woman.

Chapter 15

Elana sat, back to the wall, knees under her chin, surprising herself by nodding off. Every time, she would start to drift off, eyes closing, breathing becoming shallower and then she would jerk herself awake. She looked around the room, hoping no-one else had noticed. First time, Saran had smirked at her, but even she had stopped doing that now.

They've been gone for ages.

That was the thought that forced her awake every time. Mark could be dead and she was falling asleep. *Get a grip!* She forced herself to stand up, and rubbed her arms. She wasn't cold, not really, but it felt very cool in the room. Her legs protested, and pins and needles shot down her thighs settling in her calves.

She nudged the dresser with her arm, but it didn't move. It had taken both her and Saran to get it in front of the door in the first place. A very solid piece of oak furniture, probably obscenely expensive.

"You ok?" Saran whispered. She was sat on the bed, stroking Sandra's hair. The other woman had her eyes closed, although they were so puffy from crying that it was hard to be sure. Sandra hadn't said a word since Mark and Bruce left.

Elana nodded. "I'm just," she shrugged, no idea how to finish the sentence.

"I know, me too."

Elana sat on the bed, keeping a small distance between herself and Sandra. "Where are they?"

Saran had to lean in, so Elana repeated herself, a little louder.

"Getting help," Saran said, but her words lacked conviction.

"They should've been back by now. What are we going to do?"

Before Saran could answer, they heard a loud knocking on the door. Both of them jumped and Sandra sat up shouting, "Jeff!"

"It's me."

Elana felt relief flood through every fibre in her body. She leapt up and ran to the dresser. She pushed at it, but it didn't move.

"Help me!"

"Wait," Saran said. "What if he's not alone?"

Elana looked at her, incredulous. "We have to let him in!"

"But, if he's with them, they might kill us all."

"He's alone!" She was nearly shouting now, a stark contrast to just thirty seconds ago.

"We don't know that," Saran said.

"She's right," Sandra said. "If we let them in, they'll kill us all."

"There is no them. He's on his own."

"What's wrong babe? Open the door."

"Are you alone Mark?" Saran asked.

"Yes."

Elana shot her a look that said see? Saran shook her head. "He's bound to say that," she hissed.

"Help—me—move—this—dresser," Elana said through clenched teeth.

"We have to be sure."

"Come on, open the door, let me in." Mark started to rattle the door handle, but the door wouldn't open even an inch. "Hurry up!"

"I'm trying, hon." Elana looked at Saran with pleading eyes. "What if it were Bruce?"

"You'd be saying what I'm saying," Saran said. Her complete and utter calm was beginning to get on Elana's nerves.

"What's the fucking problem?" Mark was shouting now, but also trying not to. She could hear the edge in his voice.

"Saran, please."

Saran stood with the grace of a dancer and crossed to the dresser. Now, Elana could see the stress in her shoulders: this is not a good idea, she was saying. Elana started to push and Saran dragged. At first the dresser didn't move, but then it slid across the carpet and they had enough room to open the door. Mark slipped in quickly and helped them drag the dresser back.

Elana hurled herself at him and was about to smother his face in kisses, but she stopped when she saw the state of him. "Oh my God."

"That bad huh?"

She lifted a hand to touch the bruises, but he grabbed her wrist.

"Don't," he said.

Elana felt tears well in her eyes and hated herself for it. Mark was the one in pain, not her. His left eye was swollen so badly it looked shut, and his top lip jutted out. His mouth and nose were covered in dried blood and bruises were beginning to show. Sandra and Saran said nothing, but their faces told enough of what they were thinking. She clung on to his waist, not wanting to let him go.

"Where's Bruce?"

"We don't know," Saran said.

"He should be back by now," Mark said.

She only nodded.

"He'll be okay," Elana said, but she caught a look on Mark's face and decided not to say more. He stepped to the side, forcing her arm to drop.

"What's going on?" Saran asked after a long pause. "What do they want?"

Mark sat on the edge of the ottoman and put his head in his hands. Elana sat on the bed, trapped in a no man's land between the women and Mark. Saran had resumed stroking Sandra's hair. He opened his mouth to speak, but stopped and shook his head.

"Just tell us," Saran snapped. It was the first time her calm had slipped.

"Mark," Elana said, far more gently.

"You're not going to believe this," Mark said.

Bruce sat in the woman's blood, adrenaline making him tremble but shock immobilising him. He could not explain why the sight of the woman's lifeless gaze had shocked him but it had upset him on a profound level. Prior to this evening he would have said that there was not a chauvinistic bone in his body – quite the opposite – but the simple fact that a woman was involved in this was deeply upsetting.

A noise outside made him jump. A banging sound, like something being hit repeatedly with a hammer. *Got to move.* He tried to get up, but his legs gave way and he slipped back onto the blood soaked floor. The blood was still exploring the cracks and crevices of the kitchen floor beneath the woman and Bruce had visions of a flood of blood seeping back into the bar area.

The thought spurred him into action. He stood up, forcing his legs to be strong, but he still had to lean on the counter for extra support. His heart was hammering so hard against his ribcage that he thought it would burst through like John Hurt in that film. He still held the knife, his grip so tight his knuckles were white.

"I have a weapon," he said, only realising he'd spoken aloud when the noise made him jump. *Making yourself jump - some hardened killer you are.* The banging outside continued unabated; at least no-one out there had heard him. *Still have to move though.*

But where?

The location was so obvious that he almost physically kicked himself. It was perfect and near. His house. Adjacent to the pub, and connected to it, but not accessible from within, his home was less than twenty metres away.

He chuckled to himself, and ran a blood soaked hand through his hair. *I can get cleaned up there. Have some time to think, and get to a phone. The others, especially Saran, will worry, but this way help gets here quicker.*

The decision seemed to help him gain control of his disobedient limbs. The trembling in his legs stopped and he felt better. He crept to the back door and peered out into the gloom.

It was still snowing, but not as hard as before. The temperature was way below freezing and he knew he had to move quickly. The banging noise was coming from directly in front of him and he looked that way.

His shadow was clear on the path in front of him.

"Christ!" he muttered and stepped into the night, out of the light. He pressed against the wall behind him. Instantly the cold bit into his bare arms and head and snow settled on his hair. He rubbed his arms with his hands but succeeded in only creating pink streaks on his bare skin. "Got to get back inside," he said. *Talking to yourself, that's not good. Actually talking out loud was definitely not good.*

The path led away in front and to the left of him. The left fork would take him to the two propane tanks and generator that kept the lights on; straight ahead took him to the lean-to shed that was the wood store. Past the wood store stood the fence that surrounded the pub to protect the privacy of their kitchens and keep the wildlife out. The gate in the fence led straight on to the moor.

It was also where the banging was coming from.

"What are they doing?"

From behind him, a door creaked and he knew that someone had entered the kitchen. It would be mere seconds before his handiwork was uncovered. Nothing else for it: Bruce ran.

The snow crunched under his feet, a sound that seemed unnaturally loud and clear. He could have been shouting at the top of his voice and it wouldn't have appeared any louder. He forced himself to calm down and stop running. It was pitch black and snowing, he would already not be visible from the kitchen doorway.

He heard a shout and knew that the body had been discovered.

He reached the generator and ducked behind it. Its hum was comforting; reassuring that it continued to work despite everything happening around it. The generator and tanks were in a lean-to shed, open on one side. A small shelf at the back held a CB radio – an ancient thing that looked like it came from the early 1980s when these things had become inexplicably popular. Bruce reached a hand for it, knowing it was there rather than seeing it. The microphone came free in his hand, chord hanging loose. He felt along the top of the machine and swore to himself. The machine had been smashed to pieces.

Back to plan B.

Across the lawn, only six or seven metres away, a gate led through to his private courtyard garden. From there, a couple of steps to his back door and safety.

Nearly there.

Bruce peered around the generator, looking back towards the pub and ducked back immediately. One of the monks was standing in the doorway. He crept between the propane tanks, moving as quickly as he could without making a sound. Once more, he leant around the tank and looked at his gate.

A monk stood outside it.

Elana felt herself move away from Mark, just an inch, but it was enough to be significant. Her hand came away from stroking his back and he looked at her with his one good eye. At that point she realised how exhausted he must be. She forced herself to put her hand back, but it felt strange, like she was patting a dog.

"We're being held captive by the Devil?" Saran said, breaking the heavy silence that had followed Mark's story.

"I don't know. I-" Mark grinned, then winced, "think he's nuts, but he really believes it."

"And that means we're in trouble?"

"I don't know," he said again. "He told me he doesn't want to hurt us, he just wants us to believe."

"I don't believe in God, let alone the Devil."

"Me neither, Saran," Mark snapped.

"This is ridiculous," Elana said. "The guy is just a psycho."

"So explain how he's alive." Mark looked each of them in the eye. Only Sandra avoided his gaze. "He was shot at close range by James. Bang." He slammed his hand hard on the ottoman, making them all jump. "But he's sitting there, calm as you like. He even seems to think it's funny."

"There are drugs-" Elana started.

"I know. Maybe he's high as a kite, off his tits on crack or something." Mark shook his head. "But whatever, he believes he is the Devil."

"Do you?" Saran asked, her voice just above a whisper.

"No, I-" he shook his head again. "You weren't there."

"Come on, Mark, the Devil?"

"He knows things," Mark said.

"Yes," Sandra said and burst into tears again.

"For fuck's sake, just shut up," Mark roared.

"Mark!" Elana said.

"I've had enough, okay?" He jumped up and started pacing the room. "He knew things about my girlfriend I didn't know, okay? He knows things about you that your husband didn't know." He jabbed a finger in Sandra's general direction. "Explain that. How the fuck did he know that my best friend..."

"Mark!" Elana said, more firmly this time. He stopped and stared at her, face red. "We don't know, alright? We don't know how he knows these things."

"But it doesn't make him the Devil," Saran muttered.

"I know," Mark said. "But it was horrible down there. My friend is down there-"

"And her husband."

"My friend is dead down there. That man killed him, with those fuckers in the monks' robes. We have a problem. He will let us go, if we believe him."

117

"I'm ready to pretend," Elana said and she rubbed her stomach. "Really, if it means we can go, I'm ready to tell him anything."

"Go where?" Mark said. "We go downstairs, tell him we believe, but then what? We can't go anywhere."

"He's right," Saran said. "The question is, what happens when we tell him we believe? What does he do then? We're not going anywhere until daylight at least, and even then we might be stuck here."

"We have to do something." Elana looked between the two of them, wild eyed. "We can't just sit here."

"Yes, but what?"

No-one answered him because that was when the banging started. Sandra looked at the window, eyes wild again. Her face was so puffy from crying that she bore no resemblance to the glamorous older woman he had first seen several hours ago. *A lot has changed since then.*

"What are they doing?" Elana asked. She crossed to the window and wiped condensation with her sleeve before peering into the night.

"What can you see?" Saran asked.

"Nothing." Elana shrugged. "It's coming from over there, but I can't see anything."

"What's over there?" Mark asked.

"The generators, the wood store, the fence." Saran frowned. "Not sure what they're banging."

"The generators?" Sandra asked, voice cracking at an octave that would have most dogs whimpering.

"There's no mains electricity here. We're too remote," Saran spoke like a primary teacher addressing a year one class.

"Can they damage the generators?" Mark asked.

She shrugged. "I guess. Bruce knows more about that sort of thing than me."

"If they break them, what then?" Elana was going pale. She and Mark were thinking the worst already.

Saran's infuriating shrug again. "Then we get no light."

"Well, that's just great," Mark said. "No heat and now no light either."

"Hang on though, they'll be without heat and light too," Elana said.

"Yes, but they think they serve the Devil. I don't think they're particularly going to give a shit, do you?"

118

Elana stared at the floor. *It was not supposed to be like this. A nice weekend away in the country with Mark. I tell him the good news and he asks me to marry him. A great party with good friends. Now, James is dead. God, James is dead.* She couldn't quite believe that she had forgotten that fact, if only for a moment.

"What if we tell him we believe?" Sandra said. "He might leave the lights on."

Mark gave her a pained look. "He might. Then again, he might just kill us all."

"But you said-"

"I know what I said," he snapped. "I don't think he's going to let us go. He killed James and Jeff and we are witnesses."

"I didn't see him kill James!" Sandra said.

"No, but I don't think that will bother him." Mark sighed. "Bruce could be-"

"Don't say it," Saran said. "Don't speak those words, Mark: I'm warning you."

He stopped and nodded. He knew how she felt – he didn't want to acknowledge that Bruce could be dead, in case that somehow made it true. Besides, Bruce had to be alive; otherwise Adam would have paraded the body in front of him surely?

So where was he?

Bruce shivered and rubbed his arms again. The cold had engulfed him and all he wanted to do was lie down and go to sleep. He shook his head and tapped his own cheek to try and wake himself up. It was no use. He had to move, and move now, or he would join the growing list of corpses for the night.

He peered around the generator again. The monk still stood by the gate, unmoving. Bruce had no idea how long he had been sat next to the generator – five minutes? Ten? The banging continued unabated off to his right, punctuated by a loud crash as something fell every few minutes or so. There had been at least two of the louder bangs, so Bruce guessed that it had been nearer ten minutes.

The fence loomed ahead of him and beyond that the moor. He had never been that side of the fence, but he knew it rested against the slope of the hill up to the cairn. He had two choices: he could rush the monk and try to get into the house that way. He still had the knife and

119

so killing another monk didn't present a huge problem for him. He had killed one, what's one more? *God, is that how serial killers start?* The thought nearly made him retch. Could he really go through that again? Stabbing another human being repeatedly until they stop breathing? Kicking them until their face becomes a bloody mess? He was lucky last time, lucky that it was a woman and he was stronger. If it were a man, he would be in trouble. He was under no illusions as to the extent of his physical prowess: he was no action hero. His actions were upsetting, he could not just move on to the next one without consequence.

The thoughts made up his mind: he would go around.

He forced himself to move and crept to the fence. The previous owners had erected a seven foot solid wooden fence around the outside of the pub to stop people gawking in. It would have been very useful in the summer, but now it presented a challenge. Snow had gathered along the top of it and even settled on the cross beams. He put his foot on the lowest strut and pushed up, reaching for the top of the fence as he did so. His foot slipped and he didn't catch the fence but fell against it with a bang, sliding back to the snow. The wood rubbed his shin removing a layer of skin and forcing him to cry out.

The banging stopped. Bruce held his breath. He couldn't see the monk. Better move, and move now. Without waiting to see if he had been discovered, he tried to lever himself up again. He put his foot where the snow had been kicked away by his fall and jumped up with outstretched hands.

He caught the top of the fence with both hands and hung there, feet slipping off the strut again. He tried to pull himself up and put his feet and the fence, almost running up it as he pulled. With a grunt he cleared the top of the fence, but he had miscalculated and now he was falling down the other side.

Sandra sat upright so quickly she almost knocked into Saran.

"They've stopped," she said, looking towards the window.

Elana followed her gaze, knowing that it was futile – they couldn't see out of the window without opening it. She looked at Mark, but he was looking at the floor. He had finally stopped pacing, and was sat next to her. He wasn't hugging her or touching her, but he was close and for now, that would do.

"What's happening?" Sandra asked.

"I don't know," Elana said.

"Maybe they've finished whatever they are doing," Saran said.

"But what's that? What are they doing?" Sandra shrieked.

Mark crossed to the window and tried to look out, but as before, nothing could be seen bar the snow covered moor. "We could go down there."

"Down there? With them?" Sandra looked like she'd rather have lunch with Hitler and Pol Pot than leave the room.

"What would that achieve?" Saran asked.

"We'd know what they're doing."

"We're safe in here. I'm not going anywhere," Sandra said.

"We're not safe here," Mark stated.

"Mark?" Elana looked at him, feeling the colour drain from her face.

"They know where we are. Whilst they know where we are, we're not safe."

"I thought you said-"

"Yes," he shouted, scaring them all into silence. "I know what I said, but we're dealing with a psycho – remember? We can go down there and tell him we all believe he's the devil and then God knows what happens." Mark lowered his voice. "Or we could stay here and wait for them to come to us."

The banging resumed, but much nearer and louder now.

Someone was banging on the door to their room.

Chapter 16

The door started to bulge as it was repeatedly hit by something from the other side. They all heard a loud crack and part of the door splintered.

"They're trying to get in!" Elana shouted.

"But he told me he wouldn't," Mark muttered. He looked frantically around the room. There was nowhere to go, nowhere to hide. He moved to the side of the bed and picked up a lamp. It felt heavy in his hands, enough so that he had to hold it with two hands. He ran back to the door and stood to one side of it.

"What are we going to do?" Sandra said.

"Out the window!" Mark shouted. "Quick!"

"We-" Sandra started.

Elana ran to the window and tried to lift it. Nothing happened. She heaved again and it moved slightly. The window was the old sash design and she knew that if she could get it started it would slide open fully.

"-'ll freeze."

"Help me!"

Saran crossed to her and started to pull the window up. It opened about a foot then stopped. Cold air blasted into the room, snowflakes swirling as it did so. Saran shivered.

"It's stuck," she said.

"It's enough." Elana leant into the gap. "That's a fair drop."

The door moved in and crashed against the dresser. They all heard a howl of rage from outside and the banging started again, this time with renewed vigour. The dresser started to slide across the floor, moving into the room. Elana watched with increasing horror.

"They're coming!" Sandra yelled. Saran and Elana looked at each other. Jump and almost certainly get hurt or stay and take a chance with the monks coming through the door. Neither option was agreeable.

"We have to jump," Elana shouted.

The door moved again, and the dresser slid away from the door which opened – not fully, but enough to let a grown man through. One came now, a monk charging into the space just created.

Mark swung the lamp as hard as he could and it smashed into the monk's face breaking with the force. Tiny pieces stung Mark's hands. Further cuts on cuts, but still he recovered first and punched the monk as hard as he could. He heard a bone break and the monk fell to the floor, reassuring given the double hit of the lamp and punch. Mark ignored the pain in his hands, didn't want to see the blood seeping out of the tiny cuts. He turned to Elana and grinned at her for the first time in hours.

Another monk hit him full in the back in a flying rugby tackle. Mark grunted and fell to the floor, keeping his eyes on Elana as the monk started to punch him. The blows rained on his head and he saw her move towards him.

"RUN!" he screamed, but the world was going black around the edges. Already his eyesight was blurring, and his head thick with pain. He wondered how many times you could be hit before getting brain damage then the world went black.

Elana slapped at the monk hitting Mark, but nothing happened. The monk ignored her hits and maintained his focus on Mark. She saw Mark close his eyes, saw the blood coming from his hands and the cuts forming on his face. Bruises that had come up since the last beating were being repeatedly hit again and again. She was crying and hitting, but still the monk paid her no heed.

She heard a cry and then Saran was by her side swinging an iron on its lead. The iron hit the monk on the side of the head and he stopped hitting Mark. Another monk stepped into the room and punched Saran in the side of the head. She cried out and fell back. The monk turned his cowl to Elana and bunched his fist again. Elana stepped back and hated herself for it.

123

Yet another monk came into the room, just as the first monk stood up. He stepped forward and punched Saran again, making her fall over. He aimed a kick at her head, but the third monk stepped in the way. There was the smallest movement of the cowl, but the meaning was clear: *no*.

The monk that Mark had hit with the lamp was standing, although shakily. All four turned to the bed. Sandra screamed and jumped up. She ran to the window and nearly made it before they grabbed her.

Nearly.

Two strong hands pulled at her top and dragged her away from the window. She tried to hang on, digging her nails into the wood. Two nails broke and she tried to lash out at the monk instead. She balled her hands and struck the monk several times. Every blow connected, but even Sandra knew that there was no force behind them: she was just not strong enough. The events of the day had left her with no energy. She didn't even have the will to fight for her life.

The monk pulled her towards him and slapped her once. A large, almost comically detailed, hand print appeared on her cheek. He picked her up and slung her over his shoulder in a perverse version of the fireman's lift. The other three monks stepped out of his way, one of them pushing Elana back, further away from Mark. One of them dragged the dresser clear of the door with obscene ease.

The monk carrying Sandra left the room first, followed by the others. The final one pulled the door shut on the way out. Elana ran back to Mark and stroked his face. His left eye was now swollen to the point where it wouldn't open and he had a cut underneath it that was still leaking blood. She started to cry and hugged him, kneeling so she could rest her head on his chest.

He was still breathing. His right eye opened and he blinked several times. "Can't open my eye."

Elana shushed him and kissed him on the cheek, about the only part of his face that wasn't swollen or bruised. He winced anyway.

"What happened?"

"They took her," Saran said.

Mark tried to sit up, but could only manage it when Elana supported him.

"Sandra's gone," Elana said, "the monks took her."

"We should help her."

"They're too strong," Elana looked at the floor.

"Why her?" Mark said.

"I have no idea."

Sandra was sobbing, again. She could only see the carpet, but had a good view of the blood stains at the bottom of the stairs as they went past. Though she'd been told about James, she hadn't really believed it. *That's his blood. James' blood.* He'd been a good looking boy and she'd known from the way he looked at her that things could have happened. Maybe when Jeff went to bed, whisky sozzled as usual.

That had been a lifetime ago. Both dead now. She started crying again: her husband had died hating her. It didn't matter that the story had been true (and she'd enjoyed it and had nearly taken it oh so much further); it mattered that she would never gain his forgiveness.

The monk entered the bar and threw her into a chair. She gasped at the force, and then screamed. Adam chuckled.

"Not as good looking as I once was."

His face was a mess and he fixed her with a grin that made more blood pulse out of the wound in the side of his head. Mark had been telling the truth. Adam should not be alive.

"Mark tell you what I want?"

She nodded and forced herself to breathe deeply.

"Say it."

"He said you wouldn't hurt us."

Adam just looked at her. His good eye traced the outline of her body beneath her clothes, settling on what Jeff had always called her best assets.

"You can let me go. I won't tell anyone. Please, just don't hurt me. I'll do anything. You can have me, anything you want."

Adam shook his head and sighed, looking – despite the horrific injury – like a disappointed parent. "How can you say that? Have some pride."

She wiped a tear away. "I promise you. Please, God-"

Adam laughed. "He can't help you here. The selfish twat won't lift a finger to help millions drowning in tsunamis, killed in wars or just run over by someone who is five minutes late for work. What makes you think he'll come and help *you?*"

"Just don't hurt me." Between the sobs and deep breaths, it was becoming more difficult to understand what she was saying.

"I told Mark I wouldn't hurt you all," Adam smiled, "but I am the King of Lies."

She heard the door behind her open and four monks came in. They were in pairs. Each pair carrying a long piece of wood. They carried the wood over to the fire and soon she heard a drill start up. After a couple of minutes drilling, the monks started banging something into the wall and she heard something ripping. The carpet? She didn't turn to look at what was happening and tried to ignore everything except Adam's ruined face.

"Things have changed," Adam continued. He waved his hand, beckoning someone into the room. She heard them come in and it sounded like they were dragging something heavy. She turned in the chair, rotating in a time so slow that it seemed to stand still.

One of the monks was dragging another monk into the room. She was so used to seeing them with cowls up and faces completely hidden that it took her a moment to realise the one on the floor didn't have the hood up.

Another moment after that, recognition hit her like a ten ton truck.

Adam laughed again. "Like I said, things have changed. You've got one of mine. Recognise her?"

Sandra nodded, every inch of her numb with shock. The blonde hair, now matted with thick blood. The swollen and bloody eyes, open and staring. Blue eyes that had once been so full of life: love for the walking, love for the countryside and yes, love for her.

"Why is she here?"

"She's one of mine," Adam coughed, a tiny amount of blood coming out of his mouth. "And now you will pay."

"Why me?" she wailed. "I've done nothing to you!"

Adam leapt to his feet, shouting now. "You, and people like you, have done everything to me. You give me my power, do you not understand? Why would I want a vestal virgin? How dull are they? But you…" Adam breathed in deeply, dragging huge gulps of air into his lungs. "You think nothing of lying, cheating. The things you wanted to do to this woman, but you were too scared to follow through. You got her all hot for you then you left her hanging out to dry. You cheated on your husband and over the years you've systematically run him down and thought nothing of those men you slept with. Vows mean nothing to you or this society: I've won, but He won't admit it. People, just like you, go out of their way to fuck over those they love, and then they go to church, because that makes it alright. People on the internet, hiding behind different personas, slagging off people who have the temerity to be famous. Trolls, fanboys, keyboard warriors. Insignificant idiots looking for meaning in their desperate lives. I love it, it's taken centuries of work to create this much immorality in so many people."

The monk grabbed her then, lifting her with strong hands and dragging her towards the fireplace. Another monk helped him turn her upside down and her screams fell on deaf ears. The carpet had been ripped away around the fire place and something terrible had been built above the hole. One of the monks was holding a piece of wood in the fire and now he took it out, its end covered in flame.

At some point she had become hysterical; her throat was raw with the effort of screaming but she could not stop.

As the first nail went in she continued to scream.

As her hair caught fire, she screamed.

As she knew the end was coming, she screamed.

She did not die with dignity.

Part Four: There must be some way out of here…

"I am not going to die in a pub in fucking Devon."

Chapter 17

Bruce hit snow far sooner than he was expecting. The fence was a good seven foot high on the pub side, but with the slope of the bank, he probably only fell four. It was still enough to wind him, mostly because he hadn't been expecting the fall. He didn't cry out which, under the circumstances, was a good thing.

The snow was cold, wet and thankfully still soft. *Not long till it freezes. Then the landing wouldn't have been so welcoming.* He stood up, brushing snow off him and shivering. The hill up to the cairn loomed ahead of him, a black mass of foreboding. Snow stretched as far as he could see, but it had at least stopped for now.

He was in the middle of Dartmoor, the nearest house (other than his own) half a mile away and that was Adam's. Nearest village a couple of miles, at least, and the next town was ten miles or more. He could run for it and hope for the best. He could return with help. Or not return at all. Somebody would find him days from now, frozen blue and very dead. They would wonder why he was in the middle of nowhere in the snow in just a shirt, then put it down to crazy incomers. People were always going onto the moor unprepared for what might happen. Tourists in t-shirts had been caught out many times with sudden showers or proper downpours. No, running for it was not an option.

He put his hand on the fence and looked at the pub roof to get his bearings. The chimney was slightly to his left, so he had to go right to get to the house. Keeping his hand on the fence he walked as quickly as he could. His legs sank into deep snow and he lost his balance twice as the blanket hid deep holes beneath. Soon his legs started to ache and his thighs were burning. Despite this, no sweat ran down his back and his teeth were chattering. He tried to ignore the cold, switch his mind off. He tried to remember holidays with Saran. Trips to Greece and the Islands. He pictured the sun beating down, so hot in the height of summer that the only way to get cool was to go in the sea. Even the sand was hot under your feet. He tried hard to remember that feeling but it was no use: he was freezing. The hairs on his arms stood to attention, desperately trying to get some warmth out of the air. He rubbed his arms and was concerned at how cold his own hands felt.

He had to get inside soon.

At the end of the fence, he peered around the edge. A padlocked gate barred entry to the front of their private house. Evidently the monks had a lot of faith in the padlock because no-one stood guard there. *Finally, a bit of luck.*

The snow wasn't as deep here – the wind was blowing from the east, so the drifts were the other end of the pub and fence. It was still deep enough for his feet to sink a little, but after the effort of the last few minutes he was glad for the respite. He reached the gate in a matter of seconds and grinned to himself. The house should be warm – or at least warmer than outside. The one job they had done in preparation for the central heating was to improve the insulation in the loft.

He reached into his pocket to take the keys out. His hand felt like it belonged to someone else. Felt twice its normal size. It burned as he put it deep into his trouser pocket and actually hurt when he pulled it out.

It was also empty.

He had lost the keys.

It must have been when he fell. He swore silently. *Now what? Go back and look? Not a chance; it was dark and cold.* He could look for hours and still not find them. What if he hadn't dropped them in the snow? What if they'd fallen out of his pocket in the pub? They could be lying in a pool of blood next to the dead woman for all he knew and going back there did not seem like a bright idea. He could find a stone and smash the lock. *Great idea – all the stones were under six inches of snow, anything that could still be seen would be too big and heavy.* Also, the old lock would have crumbled in his hands – one of the reasons they had changed it the day after they'd moved in. One Xena insurance approved security lock with built in alarm later and no way in through the gate without the key. He shook his head. When he had bought that lock he had not expected it to keep *him* out. They always locked it from the outside when they were out and the gate was seldom used.

Nothing else for it but to climb the gate.

The main problem was that the fence was seven foot high, with no hand or foot holds on this side – just a sheer mass of wood. He retraced his steps back to the corner of the fence. The bank rose steeply here, evidence that it had been dug out by the previous owners so that the fence could be built. He scrambled up the bank, digging his hands into the snow to help him up. He climbed until he was level with the fence. It was about three feet away from him. Not high enough. He climbed another foot and without really thinking about it, launched himself off the hill, arms outstretched.

He hit the fence at waist level and his momentum caused him to flip over and he was falling again. He reached out with his hand and caught the top of the fence. He swung into the fence, banging loudly into it and the force made him lose his grip. He fell to the snow, tumbling over when he landed.

Bruce lay absolutely still. *Pathetic jump. Next time take a bigger run up.* Even as he thought it, he snorted. *Next time? If I live through tonight I'm not going to make a habit of jumping off mounds trying to clear seven foot fences. No, if I live through tonight I'm moving somewhere hot.*

He sat up and looked over to the pub. Either he hadn't made as much noise as he thought or the monk on duty the other side of the far gate was deaf. He raised to a crouch, keeping low like he'd seen soldiers do on TV. Bruce kept to the fence, with it running along his right hand side. The garden was dark, even with the snow reflecting the clearing night sky. Nothing moved on the other side of the garden, the gate didn't fly open and no monks came storming through.

Bruce began to relax. Maybe these monks weren't as scary as he'd first thought. Maybe they'd seen that he could fight back and they were now packing up, ready to disappear. He could return to the pub and rescue Saran and the others and be a hero. His life could certainly do with a bit more respect and being a hero would be a massive step in the right direction.

Two things happened at once.

Firstly, he heard a noise. Though muffled by the pub, it was clear what it was. Somebody, a woman if he wasn't mistaken, was screaming over and over again. Loud enough for him to hear from the rear of the pub. Somebody was screaming loud enough to wake the dead. The sound chilled him more than the snow. Secondly, the other security measure he had installed, after much badgering by Saran, kicked in. Like the lock, it was expensive and the best that they could afford.

The garden was flooded with light.

Mark hugged Elana when the screaming started. She sobbed into his shoulder, grateful for the hug, feeling guilty for the relief the physical contact between them gave her. Saran sat on the other side of the bed, eyes shut. Elana noticed the lines around her shut eyes and guessed that Saran was a lot older than she looked. Guilt rose again: *how can you notice things like that with all that's going on?* Human brains are just wired funny. The things that came to mind at the most inopportune moments. It must be why some people start laughing at funerals.

"He said he wouldn't hurt us," Mark said.

"Tell that to Sandra," Saran whispered.

"We need to get out of here," Mark continued, as if she hadn't spoken. "I'm not going to die in a pub in fucking Devon."

"A pub in Cornwall do you just fine?"

"Fuck off."

He dropped his arm and stood up, glaring at Saran. "We stay here and one by one they will come and get us and that'll be that."

"Where are you going to go?" Calm Saran was back and Mark felt his anger double.

"There must be some way out of here."

Saran shrugged. "Out of the window, or down the stairs. That's it."

Mark looked out of the window for the umpteenth time that evening. The ground still seemed so far away. *Maybe if the window had faced the side of the pub there would be a nice snow drift to jump into. And if the SatNav hadn't messed up they wouldn't be here. And if, and if.* Mark shook his head. Wishing for things wouldn't change the situation. He was on his own. Correction: they were on their own. They had to think of something – fast – because no-one was coming to save them. The only people for miles seemed intent on killing them.

"We go up."

He turned from the window. Saran had spoken, her tone one of someone who had just noticed something so obvious that they were disgusted with themselves for being so stupid.

"We can't go down. If we jump out of the window, we might be okay, but the chances are at least one of us will break something. But what then anyway? There are more of them than us. If we run onto the moor, we'll die. It's too far back to town, we'll freeze to death. So the window is not an option."

Mark nodded.

"If we just walk down the stairs, the chances are they will do to us whatever they are doing to Sandra. I don't want that. I don't ever want to find out what they did to make her scream like that. Either way we can't go down. If we stay here, eventually they will come for us. The barricade didn't hold them for long, so we can't use that to help us. Only one option left."

Mark nodded at her. "We go up. There must be an attic."

Saran nodded. "There is an attic. You get to it from the corridor at the top of the stairs."

Mark's grinned faded. "Top of the stairs?"

She shrugged. "It's a pull down ladder, so getting up will be quick."

"But?"

"But it'll be noisy."

Mark swore to himself. "We'll have to be quick."

Saran shook her head. "It'll take too long. They'll get us."

"Well, that's a risk we're going to have to take."

The room filled with a bright white light. All three turned to the window.

"What the hell is that?" Elana asked.

"It's the security light for our house," Saran said. "They must be trying to get into the house."

"How bright a light do you need?" Mark asked.

"There's lots of wildlife around here. We need to scare them off," Saran said.

Mark remembered seeing the fence loom out of the darkness and thought about pointing out that the fence would probably do a good job of keeping any animal outside. He didn't say anything.

They heard a shout from outside. Elana looked out of the window and saw a monk running down the path beneath them.

"They're running to the light," she said.

"What? Why?" Mark suddenly grinned. "Bruce."

Saran sank to the bed and held her chest like a sudden pain had crossed it. Elana had thought earlier there was friction between the two, but seeing that she knew that Saran's pain was actually relief. She had felt it herself an hour ago.

"This is our chance," Mark said. "We go now."

"But Bruce-" Saran began.

"There's nothing we can do for him now. He's on his own. Whatever he's doing, he has distracted them. We go, now!"

Without another word, he opened the door to the hallway. They hadn't put the dresser back as a barrier; it had been so futile last time. Mark looked both ways out of the door and seeing the corridor empty, he gestured back to Elana. She ran to him, then looked at Saran.

"Come with us. Please."

Saran seemed to take forever to think about it. Her mind was elsewhere, then she stood up and nodded once, her head bobbing up and down, a gesture that was part graceful and part comical.

Mark led them both down the corridor. He kept his back to the wall and walked in a crouch. There was nothing to be gained by the crouch, but it made him feel better. At the top of the stairs he looked up and saw the gloss white hatch of the attic door. He looked at Saran and raised his eyebrows. She pointed at a cupboard set into the wall that he hadn't noticed before. He opened it, wincing when the hinges squeaked a little.

The cupboard was full of cleaning products. Shelves held bottles of everything from bleach to antiseptic spray, paper towels to a year's supply of toilet paper. A Dyson vacuum cleaner sat in the middle of it, new and little used judging by how clean it looked. In the corner, resting against the join, was a long pole with a hook on the end. He took it out and carefully hooked it onto the latch at the bottom of the attic hatch. He tugged down, but nothing happened. Saran motioned with her arms, her meaning clear: pull again, but harder.

Mark did and with a loud screech the hatch opened, followed by a bang as the ladder swung down to hit the hatch. The noise echoed down the stairs and along the corridor. Mark had a brief vision of a cartoon where everything shakes and closed his eyes. *They'd better all be outside.*

Something downstairs roared.

Bruce froze when the lights came on. It was so bright, like the sun had come up in an instant. *When did we buy such a bright bulb?* He seemed to remember 500W in the description, but he had no idea it would be this bright. The light had only been fitted a couple of days ago – why hadn't he procrastinated like he normally did?

He looked in panic around the garden. It was flat and rectangular in shape. Most of it was lawn, with a solid path that went around the perimeter. A solitary apple tree sat in the centre of the lawn, its shadow stretching towards the back fence like a Disney villain. He could see the gate through to the pub as clearly as if it were daylight. A shed sat by the outside gate, with a much smaller lean-to next to it. This held two bins, a green one for recycling and a black for general waste. The shed was, of course, padlocked with a heavy duty lock. *No time to get in there.* He ran to the bins and pushed the green one to the side and slipped in between them. The smell was incredible and offensive, making him gag. Forcing the bile back down his throat, he tried to sit as still as possible. He was glad of the cold; he didn't want to think about the spiders that might live in a place like this. *Do not think that one will fall down the back of your shirt. Just don't.*

Bruce looked back in horror at the garden. The light was showing something that had not been there before: something that would give away his hiding place.

His footprints. He quickly ran back into the garden and started rubbing the snow, scrubbing away all signs that he had been there. He worked back toward the lean-to, brushing the snow to remove his footprints. From the pub, he heard shouts and knew they were coming. The lean-to was still five metres away. He brushed the snow more frantically backing away towards the darkness.

Three metres.

The voices were louder now. Shouting at each other, but Bruce paid no heed to what they were saying. Something hit the gate and it rattled on its hinges. The sound was almost deafening. He slipped between the bins again, taking a deep breath as the gate opened with a crash. The wood splintered and the gate thudded to the floor. Bruce waited in the darkness, listening and trying not to let his heart beat so loudly.

He heard snow crunch and knew that a monk was in the garden. He held his breath. The crunching snow stopped, but he had no idea how far into the garden the monk had come. At least a few steps, which probably put him by the back door to the house. The urge to look was unbearable and he gnawed his fist. Now that he had stopped moving, the cold bit deep again. His hand was freezing in his mouth, fingers already numb. The need to get warm was now urgent.

More footsteps on the snow. These came closer together, so Bruce guessed that someone was running. That meant more than one monk.

"Must be a cat or something."

"Out here? Don't be stupid."

"Alright, maybe a fox."

Bruce could feel himself getting light-headed and so forced himself to breathe. His heart still seemed to be making the same noise as a hundred bass drums. Both the voices were male. It was the first time he had heard any of the monks speak. He wasn't as shocked as when he saw the female monk lying in her own blood. *Human after all. Maybe they had a chance of surviving the night.*

"Could be." This one had a strong Devon accent, not dissimilar to Adam's at the start of the night. "Looking for food."

"Nothing here now. Must've heard us and run away." More cultured, clipped, betraying a university education, but still with a local twang.

"Let's get back inside. It's freezing out here."

Bruce heard the crunch of footsteps again and the conversation continued, but he couldn't make out what was being said. Relief flooded through him as the footsteps and words faded completely. The monks had complained about being cold – major news as far as he was concerned. Suddenly they had lost much of their power as 'mysterious beings'. After what seemed like an eternity, the light went out.

He crawled out from between the bins, keeping on all fours until he knew the coast was clear; only then did he rise into a crouch. Keeping his back to the wall once more he walked towards the back door of the house. He looked up at the security light, positioned in the exact centre of their wall. The sensor was angled towards the back fence and he gave a silent prayer of thanks that they hadn't gone for the more expensive 180 degree model. He was well and truly inside the dead zone and would remain so unless he took just one step into the garden.

He reached the back door. The cottage was attached to the pub but had had an extension built at some point. The original wall ran for about ten feet before coming out into the garden. The extension held the kitchen and, above it, what had been intended to be the master bedroom. Bruce had preferred the Dartmoor view, so his and Saran's bedroom faced the moor, leaving the bigger bedroom as a very nice guest room. He snorted: all they needed were some friends to come and stay.

And, of course, to actually survive this mess.

The back door led directly into the kitchen via a single step up. At the bottom of the step a plant pot held a very small conifer that Saran was planning on moving in the spring. For now it was their emergency key stash. Bruce lifted the pot, tilting it with one hand. The pot left a perfect circle of snow and in the middle of it lay a key. Bruce scooped it up, resisting the urge to shout with joy.

He slid the key into the lock, wincing at how loud it seemed. It was worse than coming back several hours later than planned from a night out to find your partner already in bed: every sound seemed amplified to almost comical levels. Numb fingers shook as he turned the key. They still felt on fire from the cold. The lock clicked open and Bruce almost fell into the kitchen. He pushed the door shut behind him, taking great care not to let it slam or even click shut loudly.

Warmth hit him like a brick and he sank to the floor, keeping his back against the door. Tears rolled down his face and he started to sob.

"Move!" Mark said in an urgent whisper. The ladder was half out of the opening so he reached up and pulled it down to the floor. The lower half slid smoothly to the ground. On the fifth step was a clip to anchor the two halves of the ladder together. He didn't bother to attach it. Saran stood to the side and gestured for Elana to go first. "Now!"

Elana clambered up the ladder. Her footsteps clanged on the metal of the ladder, the noise ringing out in the stillness of the corridor. They all heard a door bang open downstairs. Mark watched as Elana's feet disappeared into the darkness of the attic.

"Your turn," he said to Saran.

"And you?"

"I'll be right behind you." He tightened his grip on the pole. "But first I'm going to buy you some time." He stepped beyond the ladder and waited at the top of the stairs, holding the pole in front of him like an overlong baseball bat. *What are you doing, Mark?* He heard Saran on the ladder, and knew from the silence that she was at the top. *This is a bad idea – move!* Changing his mind about fighting the monks, he ran to the ladder. He threw the pole into the opening and clambered up the ladder as fast as he could. He was halfway up when the monk appeared.

139

It was screaming at Mark, an expression of rage so raw it didn't qualify as speech. Mark lifted his foot and the monk's hand grasped air. He pulled himself through the opening and into the cool air of the attic.

Elana and Saran stood a few metres in front of him, feet apart on the rafters. Thick insulation lay between the long struts of wood, and huge, equally thick cobwebs clung to the roof. Mark could see their breath frosting as they breathed in and out and gave an involuntary shiver. They would not be able to stay up here for long.

A familiar clang of metal made him spin. The monk was coming. He knelt down and grabbed the pole, just as the monk's head came into view. Mark swung the pole as hard as he could and it gave a satisfying crack as it connected with the monk's head. The monk reeled from the blow, falling against the hatch. His hood fell back from his face and Mark swung again. This time the pole snapped as it hit the monk's head. Mark saw his skull cave in and screamed in triumph. The monk sagged and fell out of sight.

"We need to go," Saran said. Her voice was loud in the attic, but that didn't seem to matter anymore.

"Go where?" Elana asked.

Mark ignored them both and looked out of the hatch. The monk lay on the carpet unmoving. Blood was pouring out of the side of his head and his legs were crooked underneath him.

"How do I get the ladder back up?" Mark asked, turning to Saran.

She looked stricken for a moment. "You don't. It's a pull down ladder, not pull up."

"Fuck!"

"I'm sorry, Mark. I wasn't expecting Anne Frank."

"What are we going to do?" Elana cried. "They're going to come up after us."

"No." Mark shook his head. He stood up, surprised to feel his legs shaking. *I guess killing someone has that effect on you.* He could see the monk in his periphery vision, a bloody testament to his handiwork. He swallowed bile down, wincing at the acid taste in his mouth. *The bastard was coming to kill us, he deserved it.* Mark shook his head again, but this time to clear it. Rationalising and moralising could wait. Right now, there were more pressing matters to hand.

He stepped out of the hatch onto the ladder.

"What are you doing?" Elana screeched. She didn't like how much she sounded like Sandra in that instance, but couldn't help it.

"They can't follow us."

Saran stepped past Elana heading into the attic. Her feet were on the rafters, but she still walked with confidence. Mark watched her disappear into the gloom until he could faintly make out her white shirt.

"No, Mark. Don't do this."

"I have to." He smiled at her. "If I don't, they will follow us and then what?"

"They're going to kill you." Tears were rolling down her cheeks. He could see that clearly enough. Despite the tears she looked beautiful and he felt his stomach somersault. Was this the right thing to do? Could he do something else? Anything else? He looked at the ladder and saw the truth of the situation.

"I put this ladder back up, it buys you time. It might even be enough time for you to get some help or just get away."

"But-"

"No, Elana. I have to do this. We don't have long. Another one of those bastards might be here any second. I can hide. I'll be ok."

"Mark, I-"

"I know, me too. Now go."

He jumped down out of the hatch without another word. Elana almost shouted after him, but the words died in her mouth. She felt a hand on her shoulder and jumped.

"He's right," Saran said and pulled her into a hug. "If we go this way, we can get out." She jerked her head back along the length of the attic.

"What?" Elana couldn't focus on what the other woman was saying. All she could think about was how she hadn't been going to tell Mark that she loved him.

"It leads to my house. Come on."

Elana could do nothing but stare at the opening. The ladder slid back up and then the hatch closed with a click, plunging the two women into darkness. Elana stepped out of Saran's embrace and pushed her fringe out of her eyes. She would tell Mark next time she saw him, she resolved for the second time that night.

"Ok. Let's go."

Mark clambered down the ladder as quickly as he could. When playing computer games, he had seen his spec ops guy slide down ladders by holding the sides. He didn't fancy his chances of doing that successfully. Computer games, like films, had nothing to do with real life.

He stepped over the body, resisting the urge to kick it. *Hopefully, the rest of the monks are all still outside.* He pushed the ladder back up, stretching to flick it back into the attic space. Finally he used the end of the broken pole to push the hatch back up until it clicked into place.

He felt calmer now. It was a bizarre sensation after the adrenalin fuelled evening so far. *Elana is safe. She has escaped. Not far enough, not by a country mile, but safe enough for now.*

Next he turned his attention to the body. The blood had seeped from its head and was slowly soaking into the carpet. He could see small pieces of white *stuff* in amongst the wound and realised it was bits of skull. *I smashed his brains in.* This time he could not stop the bile. He threw up over the carpet, splashing the wall and his shoes with a watery green liquid.

That's just great.

Breathing shallowly and far too loudly, he pulled the monk's cowl over his head, covering the awful, awful wound. He hooked his hands under the monk's arms and dragged him down the hallway. He stopped after five feet and revised his plan. He had planned to put him in the room he and Elana had started the evening in, but now decided to go for the nearest one. God, the monk was heavy! He dropped the monk, opened the door to the bedroom before picking him up again. He grunted with the effort and dragged him into the bedroom. The monk's head lolled back at angle it really shouldn't have and the hood fell off.

The monk had brown hair and dark eyes. He was very pale and Mark understood where the phrase 'deathly pale' came from. Mark snorted; *no demons here.* He sat on the bed, breathing heavily. His New Year's resolution had been to go to the gym more (*ok, go to the gym*) and he wished he'd done it. *Not many people's lack of resolve came back to bite them in the arse in a life or death situation.*

He ran his hands through his hair. At least his hands had finally stopped stinging. His eye was still swollen but at least he could open it a little. His head throbbed but his nose was numb, possibly broken. *What now?* Elana was safe in the attic. It was cold up there, but not as cold as outside. She should be ok until the morning. Things would look better then. He should find somewhere to hide, somewhere safe. But where?

142

He could hide in the wardrobe, but that would be too cramped. Also, if he was discovered, there would be nowhere to run and that would be that. He ruled out under the bed for the same reasons.

So, upstairs was effectively a terrible place to hide. Did that mean he should go back downstairs, find somewhere down there? A far riskier proposition: he had no idea where the monks were, apart from the one dead at his feet. Also, where would he hide?

Outside was the best bet, but he needed warmer clothes for that. He looked down at the monk and started to laugh. It was obvious when you thought about it.

After a while, she got used to the dark. Her eyes adjusted and she could make out more in the gloom of the attic. Elana walked behind Saran but with none of the other woman's grace. Twice she nearly slipped off the rafter and onto the insulation. First time, Saran had given her a smile; second she was warned that if she slipped she could possibly go through the ceiling and end up back in the pub.

After that, they walked in silence. After what felt like an age, but was probably less than a minute, they came to a brick wall. It ran across the width of the attic and Elana guessed that it marked the end of the pub. The wall didn't reach the roof, however, it stopped short about a foot from the rafters.

"Our house was an extension of the pub," Saran whispered as they looked at the brick wall. "Basically they built this onto the side of the cob and then rendered over it to make it look as if the two buildings were built at the same time."

Elana had no idea what 'cob' or 'render' meant, but she kept quiet. They didn't seem like particularly pertinent questions.

"This wall was built to help support the roof extension, but they must have changed the design at some point. The roof doesn't need supporting here, hence the gap."

"When was it built?"

"Sometime after the war. Maybe even in the 60s."

"What now?"

"We go over and through that gap." Saran smiled at her. "Ready?"

Elana didn't think she could fit through the gap. It looked very small from where she was standing with a gulf of darkness on the other side. She could see no hand holds on the wall either.

"I'll give you a leg up." Saran said and cupped her hands together, ready to push her over the wall. Elana hesitated – it was *really* dark on the other side of the wall. "Come on, we need to move."

Knowing that if she thought about it any longer then she wouldn't do it, Elana launched herself forward. Saran caught her foot and pushed up. Elana hooked her arms over the wall and scrabbled up. Stone dug into her arms, grazing skin as she pulled herself up and through the gap. She was surprised at how easily she went through. *Won't be able to do that in a couple of months' time.* She dropped down the other side, lowering herself onto the floor without thinking where she was putting her feet.

"Shit!" Elana looked at her feet as she realised what she'd done. She wasn't standing on a rafter and expected the floor to give way at any moment.

"What's wrong?" Saran appeared at the top of the wall and sprung through the gap smoothly.

"The floor!"

"Relax, it's boarded." Saran tapped the floor with her foot. "See?"

Elana breathed a sigh of relief. The attic floor was covered with thick boards, closely screwed together and into the rafters. Now that they were over the other side of the wall, the darkness had eased a little, although Elana didn't fancy moving very far.

"Stay put a second." Saran moved into the gloom before Elana could say anything. An eternity – or a couple of seconds – later, bright light flooded the room, forcing Elana to jam her eyes shut. When she opened them, the light held a comforting, almost warm presence in the attic.

Saran was standing under the bare light bulb, with the cord hanging loose in front of her face. This section of the attic was boarded and in one corner stood a neat stack of suitcases. Next to them, lining the far wall were many cardboard boxes, again all neatly stacked, inside each other where possible. Cobwebs still adorned the walls although they had been pushed back to the extremities of the room. All in all, the attic looked neater than Mark's flat.

"Is it wise to have that light on?"

"I doubt they can see it from the pub. We'll turn it off in a couple of minutes when we get out of here."

Saran nodded at a hole in the floor boards just off to her left. Elana looked at it and felt happy for the first time in hours. It was a hatch to the house. She crossed to it and they looked at it for a second, before Elana felt her happiness fade.

"How do we open it?"

Chapter 18

Mark took a deep breath and stepped into the corridor. He eased the door shut behind him, wincing as it clicked. The corridor was empty. The blood splatters from the dead monk were well hidden by the carpet and poor light. Starting to relax, he walked slowly to the top of the stairs and looked to the narrow corridor below.

Nothing moved.

He had hidden the body in the ottoman where Elana had discovered the dummy hours ago. Sweat was starting to dry on his back and under his arms, making him feel sticky and uncomfortable. *Least of my worries.* The much lighter dummy he had put under the bed. Once the monks started looking carefully through the rooms, then the body, dummy and his deception would be discovered. Hopefully, he had enough time to get out of the pub and round to the house before that happened. Elana would be waiting for him; they would escape and put this terrible evening behind them. A couple of weeks somewhere hot would be a start. *Not much of a plan, but it's all I've got.*

The staircase seemed long, even longer than when he and Bruce had traversed it earlier. Again, that walk seemed like a lifetime ago. He stepped over the blood stain that was still horribly visible on the carpet. *At least the smell of vomit has faded.* He walked to the end of the corridor, hoping he was carrying himself with more confidence than he felt.

The doorway to his left led to the kitchen and right, to the bar. He could smell something strong coming from the bar and turned towards it. He pushed the door open slowly and stepped into the room. It looked, apart from one major feature, exactly the same as when he'd had his conversation with Adam. Looking at it, he felt sick and he started to convulse. *Get a grip Mark, you'll give yourself away.* He hugged himself to stop the shaking and forced himself to look elsewhere in the room.

146

The bar still had empty glasses lined up on it. Tables were pushed to the sides of the room, clearing the space around the fire place. Jeff and James' bodies lay on the floor, but a woman's body lay next to them. He didn't recognise the body, but she wore the monks' clothes. *Who had killed her? Bruce?* He pushed the question out of his mind. It was simply not an important consideration right now.

Adam sat in a chair facing the fireplace. He was slumped over, head on chest. A bandage had been wrapped around the side of his head, but it was already seeped in red. He wasn't moving. Mark stepped closer, his heart hammering in his chest. Adam's chest rose a millimetre and sank back down. Still breathing, but only just.

Something was hanging above the fireplace. Mark had tried to avoid looking at it, but he couldn't any longer. His eyes were drawn to it with the same inevitable fascination as a child looking at a plane flying overhead.

The carpet had been pulled back and ripped in a semi-circle around the fireplace, revealing a stone floor underneath. The monks had built an inverted cross and attached it to the ceiling and wall above the fireplace. At least he now knew what the banging had been. Tied, no, *nailed*, to the cross was a body. Its head dangled inches above the floor, a charcoal mess down (*up*) to its breasts. The body was still smouldering, with smoke snaking out of it. Skin had split apart in several places and now fat – body fat – was trickling out of the body, dripping to the floor. The smell of burning flesh was almost overwhelming. Mark swallowed, even though his mouth was dry.

Sandra.

Mark's arms and legs started to tremble again and blood rushed in his ears. He felt an overwhelming urge to hit something. He looked around the room for a piece of wood, the axe, the shotgun – anything – to use as a weapon. His hands gripped the back of a chair and-

"It's not working."

Mark stopped, hands still on the chair. *He should be dead.* The door from the corridor opened and two more monks came in. He let go of the chair and turned on the spot, hoping the cowl would hide his face.

"I need another one. This one is all but used up, get me another."

His voice was deep, deeper than Mark remembered, but it also wavered a little as if Adam was spending great amounts of effort and energy just to speak. His head lolled to one side as he spoke and Mark saw a small amount of spittle roll down his chin. If he had to guess, Mark

147

would say that Adam was finally beginning to die. The amount of blood he must have lost was extraordinary – it was a miracle that the man was still alive.

If he is a man.

Mark would have snorted at the thought just a few hours ago. Adam had been right – he was starting to believe. Seeing him still alive was another nail in the common sense coffin; hearing him talk suggested that Adam had a greater tolerance for pain and blood loss than any other human being ever.

Mark felt sick when he heard the words 'used up'. Sandra had died screaming: they had all heard that. The acrid smell of her burning flesh filled the room and Adam seemed to be attempting to inhale it. The way Adam had said 'get me another' was like when Mark's father had asked him to get another beer on rugby days - before he just used to ask for the beer all the time. Before he left for good when Mark was eleven. Mark took a deep breath, gagging as the burning smell hit the back of his throat. The deep cowl must have hid his gag, because no-one paid him any attention.

Adam looked at the two who had just arrived and swivelled slightly to look at Mark. "I asked you to do something." His good eye flashed with anger as he spoke and the two other monks both bowed their heads lower. Mark copied them. *I should've swung the chair. I could have hit him and hit him and hit him. For fuck's sake, why am I such a coward?* The moment had passed. As Mark followed the others out of the room, he glanced at Sandra's burning corpse and vowed that he would not be so slow to act next time.

Bruce's hands were tingling, almost painfully, as feeling came back into them. He stamped his feet on the floor and moved into the house. The kitchen was empty, but he wasn't sure about the rest of the house so he walked slowly. The door from the kitchen led directly to the sitting room. The room was long and thin, with a small mahogany table on his left. Four matching chairs sat around it, one out from the table where he had been hours ago doing paperwork. The table was still covered with paper, a white shrine to mortgage and supply difficulties. *Looks like I needn't have been worried about this month's mortgage payment after all.* A sofa cut straight across the middle of the room, separating the two halves. A large TV dominated the room, hooked up to a satellite receiver:

an expensive purchase that he'd regretted when the mortgage statement had landed. The rest of the room was sparsely furnished, just a coffee table and a small lamp. *Nowhere for psychotic monks to hide.*

Bruce let out a sigh of relief. Exhaustion hit him like a brick as he looked at the sofa. Its large cushions invited him to lie down and sink into its soft embrace. *Need to check upstairs first, just to be sure.* A door led from the living room to a hallway beyond. This had three doors running off it: one to the toilet; one to the kitchen and the final one he had just come through. The front door stood at the end furthest from him, a solid reminder of how much insulation white plastic gives you. The stairs led up opposite the door. A couple of coats hung on hooks by the front door – both Saran's.

He looked up the stairs. It was dark. The familiar surroundings felt threatening suddenly. Dark shadows hid monks everywhere he looked. He started up the stairs, trying to keep his weight light so no step creaked. At the top of the stairs, another hallway ran behind him and three doors led off that way. In front of him, the door led to the bathroom. The door was shut, the gloss paint glistening in the moonlight streaming in from the window above his head. Behind him the hallway seemed twice as long as normal, and even with the moonlight, very, very dark. The doors to all three bedrooms were shut.

Surely the monks wouldn't hide up in the dark on the off chance he came here? Surely they would cover the doors in to the house. He had seen the one on the gate, was there another at the front door? That would make sense, but then the evening hadn't been exactly logical to date.

He opened the bathroom door. Long and thin, the bathroom was deceptively big. It was also cold. The main feature was the oversized bath, which took an age to fill but then you felt like a film star when you got in. He had planned on christening it with Saran when they'd moved in, but she had other ideas. The bathroom was empty, so he started to relieve himself, realising as soon as he started that he'd left his back to the door and was standing in a very vulnerable position. It seemed to be the longest piss of his life, but he finished without incident. He nearly flushed the toilet just out of habit but stopped himself just in time. Bruce ran his hands under the cold tap as the hot would fire the boiler in the pub. *This is ridiculous. I can't even piss and wash my hands.*

When he was done, he opened the door to the smallest bedroom, which was next to the bathroom. This room felt positively tropical compared to the bathroom. They were using it as a dumping room at the moment and it was still full of unpacked boxes. The boxes were stacked neatly around the walls, leaving no hiding places for a monk to jump out from.

He searched the other two rooms quickly and began to relax. He was alone in the house. He smiled to himself and returned to the main bedroom. The king size bed dominated the room and it was even more tempting to jump in it and pull the duvet over his head until morning. Instead, he went to the cabinet that sat beside his half of the bed. He rummaged in the top drawer and found his mobile phone. Battered and scratched, but it still worked. Bruce had never been one to have the latest model. He was about to switch it on when he heard voices.

He dived to the floor and squeezed under the bed, heart hammering in his chest again. *Would this night never end?* He held his breath and tried to focus on what was being said. The words were muffled and sounded far away. He crawled across under the bed and looked out to the landing from under his bed. *Thank god I left the door open.* He could see clearly down the corridor. The moonlight lit the hallway enough for him to see. He knew that he was safe under the bed; the darkness on the landing would help hide him from anyone coming up the stairs.

No-one came. The stairs didn't creak, but the voices continued, louder now but still indistinct. At least he could pin point them now though: the sounds were coming from above him. He moved quickly, dragging himself out from under the bed and almost running into the hallway.

He stretched up, at full reach and pushed the attic hatch up. It moved a little, but he couldn't move it more than that. Returning to the dump room, he got one of the sturdier boxes, pushing it into place under the hatch. Once on it, he reached up again and opened the hatch. Once more he held his breath – just in case he was wrong.

Saran and Elana looked down at him, terrified expressions turning to grins when they saw who it was.

Mark followed the two other monks as they went back upstairs. His heart sank and a deep dread grew with every step he took. He hadn't been able to see their faces when Adam was talking due to the dark shadows caused by the cowls, so he assumed that they couldn't see his either. However, it wouldn't matter how good his disguise was if they found the body. Could he run if they discovered him? Probably, but trying to prevent the discovery was a better plan and so he fought every fibre in his body that was telling him to run.

They walked along the corridor stopping outside the last room. The first monk kicked the door open. It smashed into the dresser and bounced back almost hitting him in the face. The monk grunted then pushed it open and moved into the room.

"They've gone." His voice was deep and tinged with a Devon accent. He reappeared at the door. "What are you waiting for? Find them!"

The last words were roared and the other monk turned so quickly he nearly bumped into Mark.

"Come on!" He pushed past Mark to the door opposite and kicked it open. He stepped over the threshold and flicked on the light, hitting the switch with an audible thump. Mark knew this was his opportunity and turned down the corridor. He ran to the end room and opened the door with a bang. He made sure the door crashed open. From the doorway he quickly scanned the room. He couldn't see the dummy under the bed and the ottoman lid was securely shut. Behind him he heard other doors being kicked open.

He racked his memory – were there three doors, or four? Five? He couldn't remember. Either way he didn't have long. He turned back into the corridor and looked for the monks. They were both already in the corridor, looking at him. One of them had pulled his cowl back, revealing the weather beaten face of a man in his fifties.

"Anything?"

Mark shook his head, having to exaggerate the movement to get the cowl to move.

"Shit, he's going to kill us."

"State he's in, he's not killing anyone." The other monk's voice was that of a much younger man, again with the twang of Devon in there.

The other man pushed the younger monk, forcing him up against the wall. "He doesn't need to be strong to kill us. Don't ever forget that."

Mark took a step forward, but the older man fixed him with a glare. "Problem?" Mark shook his head. "Good."

"We need to find them and quick. He needs a new sacrifice, or the body will give up."

"They must be outside." The younger monk pushed the other away. "They can't go far in this weather. Let's go." He brushed past the older man and stopped when he was level with Mark. He looked at the other man said, "Just so we're clear, don't ever fucking touch me again."

The older monk laughed. "Just so we're clear, don't fucking under estimate his powers again."

"Come on," the younger one said. "We've got people to find before we lose our boss."

He led the way back down the stairs. Mark heard the shuffling steps behind him and knew the other man was coming. Instead of turning into the bar, they entered the kitchen. A streak of blood led from the central island of cupboards and to the door they'd come in through. Mark faltered for a second when he saw, but carried on walking. The hem of his stolen robe dragged through the blood.

It must be the woman. Bruce must have killed her. Mark tried not to laugh; it would be a mad, delirious sound anyway. Bruce was alive! With the dead monk upstairs, that brought the number of monks down, but to what? How many were there? Had enough died to swing the balance in their favour? Probably not, for some reason twelve was the number in his head. Were there twelve monks, or was that one of those portents in literature so he just thought it was twelve? No matter; there were definitely two in front of him now. Another thing was that at least one of the monks believed that Adam had powers. Unspecified powers maybe, but powers none the less. Neither monk had called Adam by his name – what did that mean? Maybe they *did* think Adam was the Devil. It would explain why they were so quick to follow his orders. He was also weak and needed help; perhaps that could be used to help the others escape.

He breathed in sharply when they stepped out into the night air. It was so cold. The snow had finally stopped and the clouds had cleared. Ice crystals had formed on the top of the snow, glistening in the moonlight.

"You fucking sightseeing or coming?"

Mark almost jumped out of his skin. *Ridiculous, I almost forgot where I was.* He jogged past the generator lean-to and the remains of a log store. Splinters of wood littered the floor. *That's where the wood for Sandra's cross came from.*

A monk stepped out from behind the furthest building and raised an arm in greeting. The older man did the same whilst the younger monk saluted. "Nearly there!" the other man shouted. Mark saw the older man grin at this news before they were out by the road.

152

The entire road was covered in snow, the surface smooth as far as he could see. The clear skies had caused the temperature to drop further and he could see ice crystals glistening on the top of the snow. Under no circumstances would the road be useable in the morning. *We need to rethink our plan.*

The three of them fanned out, none straying far from the gate back into the pub's garden. The older man lifted his hood back over his head, shivering as he did so. "Nobody's been out here."

"Nope."

"So where have they gone?"

Eventually, after scanning the road and moorland pointlessly for a couple more minutes, they turned back to the pub. They were about to go back into the garden when the younger man stopped.

"What's that?" He was pointing down the road at the building next to the pub.

"It's the house for the owners," the older man said. "They haven't gone there, look at the snow."

Mark felt his heart sink. They had come through without discovering the body upstairs but were still going to be found out. His mind started to race: what could he do to stop them going to the house? Two of them would be too much for him to tackle and he wasn't up for another fight anyway. Talk to them and his disguise would be blown.

"They might have found another way."

The older man waved his hand. "Whatever, if you want to waste your time you go right ahead. Take Greg with you if you want, but I'm going back inside." He turned on his heel and went back through the gate.

"Come on," the other man said and started to walk towards the house. It took Mark a second to realise that he must be 'Greg' and he followed a few steps behind the other man. They passed his car, which had some snow on it and as Mark approached the boot he heard a definite, loud click as the boot opened. It swung up, causing all the snow to fall off it. Mark patted his pocket. His key was still in there and it had made the boot fully open when he got close. It wasn't supposed to do that. Another thing to sort out when he took the car back after the weekend. Mark looked in the boot, his back to the other man.

"What the fuck?" The monk turned towards the car. "Why did that open?"

Mark swung his bag as hard as he could. It connected with the other's head forcing him to stagger and fall to the ground. Mark pounced, punching the side of the man's head. The monk roared and pushed up with strength that surprised Mark. He fell backwards, stumbling in the snow and ice and landing hard on his backside. The monk tried to get up, but the snow slowed him for a vital half second. Mark launched himself forward. The rugby tackle was hard enough to make a cracking noise and they rolled onto the snow. Mark somehow ended up on top and rained more blows down on the monk.

"What are you doing?" the man screamed, but still Mark hit down until his arm started to hurt. The monk sensed that he was tiring and brought his arm free of Mark, hitting him in the side of the head. Mark felt sluggish as soon as the punch landed and could feel blood pouring out of his nose. *Well, if it wasn't broken before, it is now.* The monk hit him again, this time catching one of the many bruises around his eye and Mark fell off him. The cold snow felt comforting and Mark just wanted to lie there and go to sleep.

"What the-" the man said. "Greg?"

Mark shook his head, trying to clear it. He'd hit the monk so many times and he'd got up easily. By contrast, he'd been hit twice and was on the floor. *Definitely need to spend some time in a gym.*

"Greg, you twat. What are you doing?"

Mark was still lying face down in the snow, the cold helping clear his head now. His hand closed around a rock partially covered by snow. *No time to think.* He stood as quickly as his body would allow and swung his hand with all the remaining force he had.

The stone connected with a sickening crunch. Blood flew out of the cowl as the monk's head whipped to the side. Mark swung again, striking the same side of the head: at least this time he was causing damage. A third hit with the rock and the monk fell to the floor with a grunt. He didn't move. Mark dropped the rock to the snow. Dark shadows of blood glistened on it in the moonlight. Mark walked to his car on unsteady legs. The entire world seemed distant, like it was happening to someone else. His left eye was aching and had nearly closed again. It hurt every time he blinked. *Probably done some real, permanent damage now.* His hood had fallen down in the fight but he didn't put it back up. The open boot was dark, the illumination from the in-boot light pathetic. *Something else to moan at the dealer about.* He lifted the carpet in the base of the boot and pulled out the tyre iron.

With the detached feeling remaining, he turned back to the monk. Spitting blood onto the snow, the monk had somehow managed to get to all fours, trying to stand up. He wasn't paying attention to Mark, didn't look up. Mark walked slowly over to him and hit him as hard as he could with the tyre iron. He hit again and again until he heard the skull crack, but even then he threw a few more hits in. *Got to be sure.*

Mark sank to the snow, looking at the second person he'd killed in as many hours. Here it was kill or be killed – Sandra had shown him the truth of that. The man's hood had fallen off and blood was pooling around it. No way could this robe be stolen. Mark reached out to turn him over.

"Don't do that."

The voice should have made him jump, but it was so familiar that he drew comfort from it instead. Mark laughed. "You're dead."

"Yep, but that doesn't matter. Please don't turn him over Mark."

"Mate, it's good to hear your voice."

"I know Mark, I'm happy to be here, even if the implication isn't that good for you."

Mark laughed again. "Yeah, you're right. Hearing dead people can't be good."

"You're not Bruce Willis."

"No, man. He couldn't hear the dead people. It was that creepy kid." Mark rubbed his face. It was tender to the touch. "God, he hit me hard."

"He did, but you'll be ok. Just get to safety, just get away from here."

"I'm trying."

"Try harder, mate. Get up, stop feeling sorry for yourself. Go to Elana and get away."

"You never liked her."

"That's not true."

"Mate, you're dead, don't lie to me."

"I'm not even here Mark, so if I'm lying it's because you're making me. Don't turn him over."

Mark blinked hard and picked up a handful of snow before rubbing it in his face. It stung where the cuts had reopened, but it did make the world come back into focus. He looked around him, but no-one was there. The snow was disturbed where the fight had taken place, but only two sets of footprints could be seen leading to it. *Imaging things now, not good, Mark.*

He reached forward and turned the monk over. The man was young, early to mid-twenties with a strong jawline. His eyes were open and staring back at Mark. Blood coated his face. The side of his head had caved in – *no, not caved in, I did that* – the tyre iron cutting the skin and crushing the bone. Mark put his head in his hands. He wanted to be sick, but nothing came up.

"I love good people doing bad things."

Adam's voice as loud in his head as if he were sat next to him. *This definitely counts.*

He was winning.

Bruce was back in the dump room. He lifted boxes and opened the tops of bin bags. Unsuccessful, he kept ripping the bags open before turning his attention to the boxes. He moved boxes – all marked in big black letters that were the same height saying things like "dining room" and "our bedroom" – until he found one that had "ski gear" written on the side.

"Yes!"

He pulled the box onto the floor and ripped the top open. Parcel tape initially proved strong and stretched thinly before breaking and allowing access to the contents of the box. He pulled out two ski jackets, the first a black Helly Hansen with more pockets and zips than you could possibly need; the second, from North Face, was a pale duck egg blue, considerably smaller and neater. He then pulled out two pairs of salapettes and carried them back through to the main bedroom.

Elana and Saran were huddled in the bed, duvet drawn up around their chins. Elana had finally stopped shivering and was wearing a worried frown on her face. She had told Bruce about Mark staying behind to distract the monks, but it seemed that it was only now the true enormity of that was sinking in.

"Got them," he said, holding up the clothes.

"Good," Saran said.

"There is a problem though." Neither woman seemed surprised. It was that kind of night. "There's only two of everything."

"It's not a problem," Elana said. "I'm not going anywhere without Mark. You go, get help, I'll wait here for him."

Bruce flicked his eyes at Saran, but she didn't respond at all. "Elana-"

"No." Her voice was firm. "I'm not going without Mark."

"He may be dead by now, honey," Saran said.

Elana whirled around in the bed, tears in her eyes.

"I'm not trying to upset you."

"No, you're succeeding."

"Don't," Saran said. "You have to think carefully here. He's probably dead. No reason for you to be too."

"Ladies," Bruce began, but they ignored him.

"He's not. You don't know that. How dare you-"

"Think rationally. You know what happened to the others."

Elana in particular was beginning to sound like a five-year old who wasn't getting their own way. Eventually, and for no reason Bruce could see, they both stopped arguing at the same time.

"Look, I'll go up the hill and phone for help." He waved his mobile. "No signal here, but up by the cairn there is."

"Is it far?"

Bruce shook his head. "About a two minute walk normally, so maybe five, ten at the most in this. Then the police will be on their way."

"How, exactly, are the police going to get here?" Saran spoke as if talking to the unhappy five-year old.

"They have helicopters don't they? They'll find a way when they know what's going on." He started pulling the ski clothes over his normal clothes until he resembled a ball. "I'm a bit better prepared for the weather now, so I'll be fine." He did not mention the burning in his fingers.

Neither woman commented on this.

"Look, the pair of you should layer up in case we need to leave in a hurry. We don't know how much longer it will be before they figure out where we've gone." With those words, he left and clumped back downstairs. He pulled on ski gloves which made his phone seem ridiculously small and stepped once more into the cold, cold night.

Elana sat in the bed whilst Saran pulled on the ski clothes Bruce had left on the floor. She chewed the sleeve of her jumper and her brow remained creased in a frown.

157

"It's not a good idea to stay here," Saran said. The duck egg blue coat was fitted, but still made her look like she was considerably broader than normal.

"I'm not leaving Mark."

"I'm not asking you to."

"If I leave here with you, I will be deserting him. I'm not prepared to do that."

"We've been through this. You're not deserting him. You are saving yourself. Look, we can go downstairs, sneak out the front door and be halfway back to Princetown before anyone even knows we've gone."

"I can't do that."

Saran exhaled sharply. "What do you think will happen if we stay? Mark will come running in having foiled our attackers? Don't be so naïve."

"I'm not-"

"They have killed two people for sure. Three, the way Sandra screamed. Do you want to die like that?"

I don't want to die at all. Elana said nothing. Saran was not going to stop now she was in full flow.

"I don't. I don't want to die here, tonight, screaming. If we leave now, we can be in Princetown in a couple of hours. There is a police station there. Hell, there's a massive prison there. The police will send people out here. We can save Mark."

"Bruce."

"Yes, Bruce has gone. Do you really want to bet your life on him being successful? Both lives?"

"Mark-"

"Not him."

Elana's hand shot to her stomach. "How did you know?"

"I didn't till then. You weren't drinking earlier but were pretending to. Just a guess really." Saran sighed. "It doesn't matter. Him or her, you've got to put them first. Their life is far, far more important than yours or Mark's. If he were here he would agree with me."

"You don't know him at all. What gives you the right to speak about him like that?"

"Elana-"

"No, Saran. A few hours ago, you'd never met the guy, now you're telling me what he'd do as best for his kid? He doesn't even fucking know!"

"I'm sorry-"

"Just go." She continued to stare into space for a few seconds, then seemed to realise that Saran was still there. "Fuck off!" she screamed.

Saran looked disappointed for a moment, but then left shaking her head. Elana listened as her footsteps receded on the stairs. The front door creaked open and then a soft click told her that Saran had gone.

Bruce made good time. He crossed the garden quietly, managing to avoid the sensor on the security light this time. The fence posed no problem this time as the crossbeams were clear enough to make the climb easy. In less than a minute, he was on the bank and running for the moor.

He felt great. The fresh air blew in his face making him grateful for the warm clothes he was now wearing. His heart was pounding, but from the exercise not fear and he pumped his arms and legs to power through the snow. Years before he had spent a lot of time in the Alps, working throughout the season to pay for his skiing. He knew how to move through deep snow. Soon, despite the cold, a thin sheen of sweat coated his arms and back.

He stumbled a couple of times as deep snow hid natural bumps in the ground. It was treacherous enough climbing this bank in daylight, let alone at night through thick snow. That he didn't slip more he put down to the compacted snow helping his footing.

After about fifteen minutes, the ground started to level out and he saw the dark shape of the cairn in front of him. The ancient rock pile sat undisturbed, with a thin layer of snow clinging desperately to it. The wind was noticeably fiercer up here and small amounts of loose snow blew towards him. He hunched over, keeping low as he ran across to the stones. No sense in standing upright so close to the brow of the hill; in this light he would easily be seen by anyone looking up. He rounded the stone pile and crouched down, sheltered from the wind.

He took the phone out of his pocket and unlocked it. A photo of the pub slid into view and he tapped the screen to make a call. Nothing happened. With a groan, he took his glove off and tried again. The number pad appeared. He pressed 999 and the call button.

"Please state whether you require police, ambulance or fire department." The voice belonged to a BT operator.

"Police." Bruce waited, leaning into the cairn as the operator transferred him.

"Police emergency. Call logged from mobile phone number 07955080936. How can I help?" The female voice was calm and very professional. Through her voice, she oozed confidence and it rubbed off on him.

"My name is Bruce Singer. I am stuck near Dartmoor and my friends have been taken hostage by a group of people. Two of them have been murdered, please send help." He was proud and amazed at how calm he sounded.

"Sir, where are you?"

"We're on the road from Princetown to Moretonhampstead, the only pub on that road. Hurry." Bruce rattled off the postcode.

"Sir-"

"Now, goddammit, send someone now, before anyone else dies."

"Please stay as calm as possible. We will get help as soon as we can. When did this happen?"

"Tonight, no more than a couple of hours ago."

"Where are the assailants now?"

"They're in the pub, I think. They don't know we're out."

"We? Who else is with you?"

"Three of us have managed to escape, but Mark is still with them."

"Mark? Ok, anything else you can tell us?"

"The leader is man called Adam Watson. He lives in the cottage just down the road from here."

"We are dispatching a unit now. A helicopter is enroute and there is an armed response unit on board."

"Thank you, please hurry."

"What are they armed with?"

"I don't know. An axe and a shotgun at least."

"How many are there?"

"I'm not sure. Ten or eleven, I think." Bruce didn't think this was a good time to say he'd killed one of them.

"Okay, can you stay on the line?"

"No, it's too cold and I'm worried they'll find me or my wife."

"I understand Mr Singer. Is there a safe place you can hide?"

"Yes. The house next to the pub. They haven't come near it."

"Do not approach the assailants under any circumstances. Keep yourself safe. We will be there soon."

"Oh, God, thank you. Thank you very much." Bruce hated how desperate he sounded. "Please hurry."

With that, he put the phone back in his pocket. He was grinning from ear to ear and relief was rushing through him like a tsunami up a beach. They were going to survive, goddammit, they were going to live to see the morning.

The cold was now beginning to make it through his protective gear and he felt the tips of his fingers start to tingle. *Is this what frostbite feels like?* He rubbed his hands together, the thick gloves making it an almost comical gesture. Then he had a vague memory of reading something where you weren't supposed to rub cold fingers: something to do with rubbing the ice crystals that were forming in your cells and making it worse. Bruce clapped his hands together instead and this time the gloves helped by dampening the sound.

His feet had gone numb at some point during the phone call. He had to get back and tell the others the good news. With luck, Mark would be ok too. He crept back to the edge of the hill and lay flat in the snow, peering over the brow to look down at the pub. It was all still down there; only footprints in the snow suggested that anyone had been down there at all.

He started down the hill, keeping low. He was hoping that the monks wouldn't come out as he clambered down from the brow of the hill. If it was bright enough for him to make out footprints below, then it was certainly bright enough for the monks to see a moving figure on the hill. As he made his way down, shadows engulfed him and the tsunami rushed over him again. Still grinning he upped his pace and soon reached the bottom of the hill.

Running alongside the fence were the tracks he had made on his first trip and then back to climb the hill. Next to his own tracks were two further sets of footprints. One of the sets was almost twice as big as his: no way could they be Saran or Elana's. He heard a crunch of snow behind him and whirled quickly.

161

A monk came from the side of the fence. He had been totally hidden by the shadows but now rushed forward. Bruce backpedalled a couple of steps and started to turn whilst running. He stumbled and slipped before hitting something hard. He crashed onto the snow with a grunt and the air was knocked out of him.

Standing in front of him was another monk. He was easily more than six and a half foot tall and he appeared almost as wide. He was chuckling as he turned his cowl to face Bruce. He pulled it back, revealing a surprisingly young face. The man couldn't be more than twenty.

Bruce kicked up with his foot, aiming directly between the man's legs. The big man doubled over immediately and Bruce kicked again, this time aiming at his head. Blood flew out of the man's mouth as his head whipped round from the force of the kick. Bruce stood up, just in time to be rugby tackled by the other monk. They both ended up in the snow, but Bruce responded first. He rolled as they landed, twisting his body so he ended up on top of the monk. He rained blows down on the man's head, screaming insults with every punch.

Over his shouts, he heard the footsteps of the big man just a fraction too late. He looked up in time to see the man swing his club sized arm. The blow connected to the side of his face and a white flash accompanied the bang of the hit. Bruce went cold and his vision blurred; he had never been hit so hard in his life. He fell off the other monk, lying in a heap in the snow. Even the cold and the thought of another hit couldn't make him move.

"He's mine."

Bruce blinked back tears. Both monks were standing over him now and the smaller one was holding a rock. Before Bruce could do anything, he lunged forward, swinging the rock to hit the side of his head. Bruce saw stars again that quickly faded to black. The world swam in and out of focus for a few seconds as he was hit again and again.

In the distance he could hear the steady thump-thump of an approaching helicopter.

The monk raised the rock in line with his own head and dropped it.

Bruce didn't have time to scream.

Sweat was pouring off Mark by the time he dragged the body to the other side of the road. A small bank ran away from him, down into

162

the darkness, but there was a large hump to get over first. With a heave, he managed to pull the body over the hump. He sat in the snow, breathing heavily. His eyes still threatened more tears and he punched the corpse in the stomach out of frustration. Its expression didn't change.

It was very dark where he sat and he peered back towards the pub. He could see the lights burning in the windows and the small pools they cast on the snow directly outside. Nobody would be able to see him out here. He looked out towards the moor. Even with the bright light of the moon and stars, the moor was full of shadows. Plenty of places to hide a body.

He dragged the corpse further. The going was easier now as he was heading downhill. A small concrete outbuilding loomed ahead of him and he dragged the body towards it. The building seemed to be some kind of sewage outhouse. Icicles dangled from the roof and there was no doorway on the building. The whole structure was only six feet tall at its highest point and Mark had to duck to drag the body into it. It reeked of urine and faeces and he got out as quickly as he could, retching as he returned to the cold, fresh air.

He heard a noise from near the pub and turned in that direction. It had sounded like a cry or a sob. He moved quickly, all thoughts of what the monks were doing pushed aside for now. Scrambling up the slope, he kept low, pulling the cowl over his head. Once at the top, he lay on the bank and risked a peek over the top. What he saw took his breath away.

The silence in the room was almost unbearable. The moonlight streaming through the window cast shadows in every corner. Even the end of the bed seemed distant and threatening now she was on her own. The wind suddenly howled around the outside of the house, a high pitched screaming that terrified her even though she knew exactly what it was. The wind died down almost as quickly as it had started and silence descended again. She heard things click and creak all around her and she turned her head frantically trying to find the source of the sounds. *It's an old house, lots of things just creaking away, nothing to worry about.*

Except she was in the new extension. The modern extension where you could almost smell the paint. There shouldn't be any noise.

Elana stepped out of the bed and shivered. She could see her breath steam the air in front of her.

She was already regretting the way she had spoken to Saran; *hormones playing up*. At the same time, the insane calm of the woman was infuriating. How could she be so unemotional about Mark? The answer was simple: Saran didn't know him. It was pretty easy to be callous about people you've only met a couple of hours before - regardless of how intense those hours had been.

The cold was all pervasive now so she started going through the wardrobe. Finding a shirt, she pulled off the thick jumper before quickly buttoning the shirt and pulling the jumper back on, just as she started to shiver. Next she pulled on a long cardigan, forcing it up over the thick jumper. Hugging herself for a second helped ease the cold.

She crossed the landing, entering the spare room where Bruce had found the ski gear and rummaged through the open box. The only thing she could find was a pair of electric pink ski gloves that were far too small. *Better than nothing.*

A loud thump sent her heart into overdrive and she jumped. A quick look around the room revealed no good hiding places so she cowered behind one of the larger boxes. *Stupid, not even a five year old playing hide and seek would be fooled for long by her hiding place.* But she couldn't move. She stayed for a few minutes, until her thighs began to burn, but there were no more sounds, no thumps. Peering around the box, all she could see was the same room, empty apart from the piles of boxes and bags.

She stood, her joints clicking. No movement anywhere in the house apart from her. What was that thump? The skylight was clear now and it was letting the most glorious starscape light the hallway. She realised that snow must have slid off the roof. Why didn't she go with Saran? *Stupid, stupid, stupid.*

Warm in the layers of clothes she started to move down the stairs, hoping that it wasn't too late. Saran had mentioned going out of the front so she ran to the door and yanked it open. The road was pristine, smooth snow apart from a large patch that was disturbed near Mark's car. Tracks led off towards the darkness of the moor opposite the pub. The boot of the car was open, but even at that distance she could see it was empty. Even Mark's bag had gone. The sight made her pause. What had happened there? Had they now taken his bag? Why? James' bag was gone also. The disturbed snow had a dark patch in it, roughly circular. With a start she realised she was looking at a patch of blood.

A low cry escaped from her lips. She stumbled forward, towards the car. Thick snow crunched under her feet as she staggered. Too deep to drive anywhere. She sank to her knees by the pool of blood and stretched out a gloved hand to touch it.

"No," she whispered.

A sound made her whirl around towards the moor. Something hard hit her from behind and the snow faded to black.

Mark bit his cheek to stop himself shouting when he saw Elana kneeling in the snow. He did shout as the figure moved from the shadows. Elana tumbled face down into the snow, crumbling like a puppet whose strings had been cut.

He leapt up and stepped into the road before he really knew what he was doing. Two steps forward, then he stopped. The other monk looked at him. Mark clenched his fist, ready to swing when another two monks came around from the left hand side of the pub. They were dragging a figure between them.

Outnumbered. I can't take another beating. His face still throbbed, although he could at least partially open his bad eye again.

"What are you doing over there?" a deep voice asked. Mark shrugged, pointing at Elana. "Someone stole your tongue? Help me move her. He wants more in there."

Mark crossed the remaining distance and found himself holding Elana's feet as he and the other man carried her back into the pub. His heart sank with every step; yet another opportunity missed.

"What's that?" The monk stopped just by the front door into the bar. He looked up at the sky. Mark heard it then to: the unmistakeable sound of a helicopter coming closer. Mark grinned, hoping his face was fully hidden by the cowl. Someone was coming. Help was finally on its way.

"Helicopter," one of the monks behind them said. "Quick, get inside."

They hurried through the door. Adam was still sat in the chair, looking at the fire and the burnt carcass hanging above it. He gave them a cursory glance before waving his arm at the two chairs next to him.

As they carried Elana, Mark's mind was in overdrive. Two chairs had been set out since he'd last been in here. How did they know that two people would be brought in at the same time? There were four of them still alive – why only two chairs? Coincidence?

They set Elana in one of the chairs and she slumped forward. Mark held her up, pulling under her armpits until she stayed upright in the chair. A low moan escaped her lips, but she didn't open her eyes. *She's alive, thank God!* He stepped back towards the bar, as far away from Adam as he could get without raising suspicion.

"He's dead," Adam said. "You were told to bring him to me." He raised his gaze to the smaller of the two men carrying the other body. The man flinched slightly. "I needed him alive." Adam moved with a speed Mark did not think him capable of. He grabbed the smaller man's head in his hands and twisted quickly. Mark winced at the cracking sound and the man sank to the floor. Adam breathed in deeply and returned to his chair. The ruined half of his face remained in shadow.

You should be dead.

Then Adam looked straight at Mark and smiled.

"Nice try, Marky Mark. You nearly got away with it."

Rough hands grabbed him from behind and before he could struggle, he was held in a bear hug. He was lifted a couple of inches off the floor and his legs wind-milled as he tried to get away. Strong hands pushed him into the second chair and someone smacked the back of his head. His cowl was dragged back, pulling some hair out in the process and he was punched in the side of the head again. Fresh blood ran down the side of his face and his eye closed yet again. He felt sick.

"We heard a helicopter," one of the monks said.

"Yes. We will need to deal with that." Adam still had his gaze fixed on Mark. "You know what to do." He waved his hand at the two men stood by the two corpses. Mark looked at them with his good eye, and finally accepted that the other body in the bar was Bruce. A tear rolled down his cheek. *The police have to hurry.*

Another blow landed on the injured side of his face and the room went black.

Saran had not got very far: the going underfoot was very tough. At most she was one hundred metres away from the house. A snow covered bank was on her right, so she clambered over it. From this vantage point, she could see the side of her house and the back of Mark's car. Its boot was open and the car was going to need to be dug out before it could go anywhere. With the snow clothes keeping her warm, she decided to wait for Bruce. *Ten minutes. I can give him ten minutes.*

She saw Elana come out of the house and was briefly elated: the woman had seen sense. Elation faded rapidly as she saw the monk, saw him hit Elana. Impotent rage gave way to shame as she remained hidden in the shadows of the snow bank. She peered over the top of the bank, but couldn't see anyone. Elana had gone. Saran bit back a cry. *Why didn't you help? Do something?*

At that moment she heard a *thump thump* getting louder and louder. A helicopter roared overhead. Saran punched the air, and her shout of joy was swallowed by the pitch of the helicopters engines as it circled the pub. Bruce had done his job. Help was here. She scanned the line of the hill, trying to see him. He should have come back down by now, should be by the house.

The pitch of the helicopter engines changed again as it hovered near the pub. It sank to the ground, kicking up a huge amount of snow as it did so. The blades started to slow down and the doors opened. Four men, in police blue, got out of the helicopter and fanned out in a rough semicircle. All were armed.

One of them edged towards Mark's car and touched the dark patch on the snow. He said something and the others moved apart more. One turned towards the moor and the other two ran to the wall of the pub. The first man, the inspector, used the car as a barricade. He was pointing his gun at the pub.

What happened next was so fast that she didn't believe it until it was over. The man looking at the moor didn't seem to register the dark shape that rose in front of him until it was too late. His gun was pushed into the air by the monk that had suddenly appeared. The monk dragged his arm across the front of the policeman's neck and a dark mass sprayed out covering the monk. *His blood. He's just had his throat cut.* The man fired two rounds helplessly into the air and then sank to his knees, clutching the front of his throat. Blood continued to pour from the wound, covering the man with his own blood and he keeled over.

The inspector turned at the gunshots, raising his gun but he didn't have time to fire as the shape ran off. Something reached from under the car and pulled at the inspector's foot and he fell hard onto the snow. The shape scrambled out and was on the man before he could get back up. In one hand the shape was holding a crowbar. It was raised now, glinting in the moonlight. Saran opened her mouth to scream but one of the other policemen must have heard the noise from his colleague. A single gunshot rang out and the monk fell to the snow, dropping the crowbar.

The policeman in the snow started to get up. Saran imagined him saying thanks, but then he staggered backwards. The echo of a much louder shot rang out. The policeman who had fired stumbled forward into the man he'd rescued, and then he fell to the ground. The inspector looked up at the top floor of the pub and then the back of his head exploded as a bullet tore his skull apart. The remaining officer fired at the window, but his angle was too severe and the shot ricocheted off the pub wall.

In all the noise and confusion, he didn't hear the return of the monk who had taken the first policeman. The monk scooped up the crowbar and swung it hard into the policeman's head. Saran heard a grunt, the policeman staggered, dropping his gun. The crowbar swung again and this time the policeman fell to the floor, leg twitching. The crowbar flew several more times, each thud of bar on skull being rewarded with another twitch of the man's leg. Eventually the monk stopped and there were no movements from the police at all. The monk spat at the body then waved up at the window. He walked back towards the pub and she could hear him whistling as he went.

She looked at the helicopter and saw another monk walking away from it. He had slung a shotgun over his shoulder and was whistling to himself as he walked.

Saran stood by the bank, hand over her open mouth too shocked to scream or even cry. Salvation had just been slaughtered in front of her eyes. She walked in a daze back towards the pub, half staggering in the snow. She reached the helicopter and stopped. The door was open and two men sat inside. Both had been shot at point blank range. Neither was in uniform, but both were clearly dead.

A radio sat in the centre of the console and she picked up the handset. No sound came from it. She flicked the switch on the side of it, but still no sound. She pressed a button on the head unit. It was inscribed with the power switch. Static instantly filled the cabin. Saran winced at the volume of it, but there was no-one to hear it apart from her. The monks were now safely ensconced back in the pub.

She pressed the button on the side of the microphone again. "Hello?"

"Who is that?"

The male voice made her jump.

"My name is Saran Singer."

"This is a secure channel, Ms Singer. Please put Hawkey on."

"I don't know who that is."

"It's his helicopter you're sitting in."

"Then he's dead."

"What?"

"He's dead. You need to send more help. Lots more."

"Slow down. Hawkey's... dead?"

Saran nodded before remembering that the man couldn't see her. "They're all dead. Please help me." From nowhere, tears welled and she choked in the act of saying 'me'.

"Ms Singer, how many people are we dealing with here?"

"I don't know. Some of them are dead. One of your policemen hurt one of them, killed him I think, but I don't know how many are left. They've killed lots of people tonight. You have to help me."

"We will get as many units to you as we can as soon as we can. You are our priority now, Ms Singer. Can you find somewhere to hide?"

"I don't know. I think so."

"Try to get your head down somewhere. Help is on its way Ms Singer, I assure you. Whoever has done this will not escape justice. Can you give us numbers?"

"I don't know. There were twelve, I think, but I don't know how many are left."

"And what weapons do they have?"

"Guns, crowbars, knives – anything I think. Hurry, you must hurry."

"We are on our way. Please, stay safe and don't do anything stupid."

Saran put the microphone down and looked around the cabin. At the back sat a long narrow locker. She opened it and saw a pump action shotgun. The police were on their way, so she should have been feeling safer. The shotgun glinted at her in the bright moonlight. *How long will it take them to get here? An hour? More? They won't rush in this time now they know the threat is genuine.* Next to the shotgun sat a packet of shells. *If the monks come back to the helicopter, they will find me. There is nowhere to hide out*

169

here. She could go and look for Bruce, maybe even find Elana. If she was going to try and rescue Elana, then the shotgun would give her serious leverage.

But why risk my life for someone I didn't even know yesterday? Elana was now with the monks, which hadn't ended well for anyone so far tonight. She's almost certainly dead already. I'm better off waiting here for Bruce. I've got a gun if anyone else turns up. I'll just wait here, it's the sensible thing to do.

Whilst these thoughts were going round her mind, she kept her gaze resolutely on the floor of the helicopter. Now, she raised her head slowly and gazed at her reflection in the cockpit window. She blinked back at herself, full of the quiet assurance that she had acquired through years of being self-sufficient. The person she was looking at was an older version of the one who had once campaigned against the closure of a women's refuge; gone on marches about the unfairness of fees for university students; completed several years as a volunteer on the Samaritans phone lines, enduring night after night of horror stories about just how low some people can get. That person would not sit back and let others suffer. That person would be full of righteous anger about what was happening in this pub right now. That person would not hide and let a pregnant woman die if there were a chance of saving her.

She picked up the gun and cartridges and stepped out of the helicopter.

Part Five: Reunited

"Don't do this. Please, don't leave me alone."

Mark opened his good eye and tried to take in the scene in front of him. His other eye had finally given in to the abuse it had suffered and refused to open. He could not remember having ever been in so much pain before. One side of his face was throbbing – actually throbbing - and his ribcage felt like someone had used it to practise karate kicking. The small of his back ached as if he'd been standing in one spot for three days.

But the physical pain was not the worst of it.

Adam was sitting in front of him, head cocked to one side just as he had all those hours ago. The ruined side of his face was hidden in shadows. *Has it really only been a few hours? This evening had lasted longer than several lifetimes.* Sandra still hung behind Adam, although thankfully she was no longer on fire. Her black carcass had streaks of red flesh running through it, as if someone had torn strips off her like a roast chicken. Mark didn't want to think about that. The fire burned brightly, filling the room with warmth and the smell of wood smoke almost masking that of burning flesh.

Almost.

Two monks stood either side of Adam, one of them enormous. He was wide enough across the shoulders to have to turn sideways through doorways. A huge ginger beard adorned his otherwise hairless head. A scar ran down the right hand side of his face, ending in the corner of his mouth. He was grinning at Mark, mouth slightly open. Mark had never seen anyone so truly terrifying in all his life. The other monk was smaller, but not by much. His face had a blank emptiness about it that Mark had always associated with the not-very-bright. *Numpties, James had always called his slower students. Probably not a technical term.* Thoughts of James brought a lump to his throat.

Mark turned his head to look over his shoulder at the bar. Another monk stood there, the one that had been upstairs with him earlier. He was glowering at Mark. *Can't blame him.* Three monks in the room. *Is that it? Only three of them left now. Not a bad innings from us lot then.*

Elana sat next to him, eyes wide with fear, sweat plastering her hair to her head.

"Hi babe," he said with as much bravado as he could muster. His voice sounded small and pathetically weak: not the effect he was going for.

"Mark." Now the tears came.

"Bruce must have got to the phone. Right?"

"No, they've killed them, killed them all."

"Killed who? The police?" Mark was trying to be incredulous, but he didn't have the energy. "How do you know?"

"I heard a helicopter. Gunshots," she sobbed. "Everyone's dead Mark, except you and me."

"They'll send backup, babe, we'll be okay."

"Listen to the young lovers lads, so full of hope even when there is none."

"Fuck off," Mark said, glaring at Adam. "You're a fucking psycho, I was right all along. You may have fooled the others but you're not going to carry on with this-" he searched for the right words- "fucking charade." Not the right word after all.

"Ah, but you were the first believer outside of my monks, Mark."

"No, you fucking idiot."

"Stop swearing Mark, you're usually far more eloquent than this."

"I just killed because of you."

"What?" Elana said.

"I have killed two men because of you. Two men who have been fooled into whatever shit you're trying to sell them."

"Mark, please-"

"Sshh, honey. I don't believe him. He's full of shit. I don't know what the plan is, but it seems like a game, doesn't it? Only it's gone horribly, horribly wrong."

Adam said nothing, just stared at Mark through his good eye.

Mark nodded. "You have no power. I've been thinking about this all night. These monks are just people, just like you and me, but in fancy dress."

The large monk took a step forward, but Adam waved him back. Mark breathed a sigh of relief.

174

"That story about you and James. It was famous in our circle. I'll bet good money that one of these twats heard the tale, probably up in Huntleigh with Pasty. What was it, Adam? You had a few beers and decided to wind up some grockles?"

"That's a Cornish word, Mark. I thought you were an educated man."

"It's clever that accent. You had us all fooled into thinking you were some kind of bumpkin when we first got here, but now we know it's all an act. What do you want, Adam, what do you want from all this?"

"I don't understand." Elana said, looking from Adam to Mark. "James didn't remember me."

"There's a dead woman too, and I'll bet my fucking savings that she was Sandra's lover," Mark continued, ignoring Elana. "Did you ask her to seduce Sandra, just for this day?"

"Mark, Mark, Mark." Adam shook his head, slowly, keeping the side of his face ensconced in shadow. "At what point did you assume I was telling the truth? I am the Prince of Lies, the Destroyer of Truth. I will use all methods at my disposal to do that."

Mark saw a look pass between the two monks behind Adam; not enough yet, but seeds of doubt had been sown. He pushed on, his voice gaining strength as he spoke.

"Pasty was with James the night they went to Swansea. Pasty probably watched whilst James had his fun with Elana; everything was just funny back then, all about the story. I swear sometime the nights out were funnier in the retelling than they were in the living. To Pasty it was just another tale, a brilliant story, until we met again. I had no idea, and I don't think James did either. He was like that you see, no memory for women and they always came easily to him. Sorry, honey. I bet after we came down a couple of weeks ago that Pasty was talking in his local about how funny it was that his mate was seeing a girl that had once been naughty in a nightclub."

Uneasy shuffling now, between the two disciples. Mark didn't dare look at the other one. "And Sandra, poor, poor Sandra, bored shitless married to Jeff, and who can blame her? He was boring and she was an attractive woman. The woman you sent, it must have been so flattering, so nice to be wanted by someone. Another of your big secrets ruined, revealed to be a parlour trick, smoke and mirrors. You're a fucking fraud, face it and lots of people have died tonight because you're a nutter."

Mark was breathing hard now, sweat trickling across his brow. Elana was open mouthed, stunned at the way Mark was speaking. The big monk was almost foaming at the mouth.

"That's really good Mark. What am I supposed to do now, say I would have got away with it if it weren't for you meddling kids?" Adam laughed, but no-one joined in. "Tell me, Mark, in all of this scheming, how I managed to make sure you were all here this evening? Did you plan to come here? The look on your face says it all. I knew you'd be here, along with the lovely Sandra here. She makes a wonderful addition to the bar does she not? What a feature! They'll be talking about her for the next two hundred years."

The monks were smiling again now, nodding along with Adam. Mark felt like the funny kid in school who had managed to get some laughs from the bully's gang before getting his head kicked in anyway.

"Tell me Mark, come on, explain how I knew you'd all be here."

"Tom had a party this weekend, and for all I know, Jeff was in on it and dragged Sandra here. You killed him to keep your cover story going. Pathetic really."

"That's good Mark. You should try screenwriting. But tell me this, if I am not who I say I am, and if there is a rational reason for everything that has happened tonight, explain this."

Adam leant forward, letting the light play across all of his face for the first time since Mark had awoken.

"Sacrifice makes me strong, Mark. I'd say young Bruce there had a few skeletons in his closet, as did the young men and women of the police force outside."

Adam's face had entirely healed. What had once been an empty socket and shattered cheek was now pink skin and a piercing blue eye. Mark recoiled from the gaze as Adam began to laugh.

Elana was on the verge of hysteria. She could feel a tightness develop across her chest and the air seemed to be sucked out of her lungs. Adam was entirely healed, which was impossible. Mark had said earlier that he had been shot in the face: either Mark was lying or Adam had healing powers that would make superheroes jealous. His laugh was deep and full of bass, entirely like an old school film villain. Her legs started trembling and she was glad she didn't have to rely on them at that precise moment.

She also found it hard to look at Mark. He had killed two men tonight. Twelve hours ago, Mark was just the father of her child and a man she loved without question. Now he was a killer. *Self-defence, right? How did he do it? With his bare hands?* Those hands had been touching her earlier in the day. The tight feeling in her chest intensified.

"Mark." Her voice sounded far away. More urgently: "Mark"

He turned to look at her, just as she slid off the chair away from him. Her entire body flopped onto the carpet and she clutched at her throat, gasping for air. *This is it, I'm dying, right here, right now.* The Fatboy Slim song sprang into her mind, running round and round as she tried to gulp down air like a fish on the deck of a boat. Dark spots formed at the corners of her vision and the room started to blur.

She began to convulse. Her entire body was shaking and she could feel saliva streaming out of the corner of her mouth. Mark moved to her side, but one of the monks grabbed him and tried to pull him away. Mark stood quickly, swinging his fist into the man's face. The monk let go as Mark followed his punch with a head-butt. The largest monk stepped forward, but Mark ignored him and knelt next to her again. She could feel him turn her onto her side as he moved her into the recovery position.

Adam held up a hand again and the giant stopped. The other monk was holding his nose as a distressing amount of blood poured out of it.

"Love's young dream," Adam said with a smirk. "You don't mess with that."

Mark turned to face him, but Adam was talking to the monk with the broken nose. The monk was pinching the top of his nose, but it didn't seem to be slowing the blood.

"She'll be alright," Adam continued, now turning to Mark. "It's the baby you should worry about."

"Baby?" Mark said, sitting on the floor. Elana's convulsions were slowing now and then stopped altogether. She blinked at him as the horrible rasping sound of her breathing slowed.

"What happened?" she said.

"You had a fit. Just lie there for a minute." As soon as the words were out of his mouth, the monk with the broken nose hit him and he fell over, ears ringing.

"We'll give the orders around here," Adam said. "Put her back in the chair." The monk kicked Mark in the ribs, then pulled Elana up.

At first he tried to pick her up by the arms, but she screamed and wriggled away from him so he grabbed a clump of her hair and dragged her onto the chair. She screamed again, holding her hair where he was pulling and when he let go, a clump of strands fell out of his hand. He smirked at her.

Mark rolled over and returned to his own chair, clutching his ribs. He didn't look at the monk, but glowered at the carpet. He reached out and squeezed Elana's hand.

She smiled at him through the tears. "Sorry."

"You ok?"

"Will you two just shut the fuck up?" snarled the giant.

"I love you."

"I know." Mark smiled; his favourite Han Solo line. "You're pregnant?"

She nodded, giving him her full attention despite the many distractions in the room.

"That's brilliant news," he said, his smile broadening.

"Well, if you two are done being all lovely to each other, maybe we can get back to business," Adam said.

"What do you want?" Mark said. His mind was still reeling from his cracked ribs and the fact that Elana was pregnant. *There must be more police coming. Must be. I just need to stall him long enough and find a way to get Elana out.*

"Oh, I would like an end to wars and famine and for everyone to just learn to get along," Adam said, in a falsetto. He paused and laughed, looking at each monk in turn before resting his gaze back on Mark. "That's a lie obviously. If that happened, there'd be no need for me."

"I don't think we need you," Mark said.

"Go on then, Mark, explain yourself."

"There's enough hurt and suffering in the world without any need for the Devil."

Adam mimicked his words in the same falsetto and laughed again. No-one else in the room joined in. "Really, please, go on."

"If you really are the Devil, then what is your game? What do you want? Why are you here? What are you trying to achieve? Some people are dead tonight because of you, four on our side" -he winced at Bruce's body- "and the same on yours I think. Well done. Superb

178

attempt at sending the world into darkness. Eight dead! Fuck me, more people die of the flu every winter than you've managed tonight."

"Excellent points, Mark, all of them. Really, I applaud your thinking. Please continue."

"I always thought you'd think a bit bigger than this. Really, Bin Laden accomplished more in half an hour with a couple of planes and some willing volunteers than you have tonight. You want the world to believe there's a Devil? A real-life Devil? Not a chance, we already have them. All the rapists, murderers, paedophiles, dictators. All of them – they're all worse than you. You are fucking small fry in comparison." Mark was breathing hard now. He touched his face and winced.

Adam actually applauded then. "Oh bravo, Mark, quite the performance. What a speech! Now, let me take your points and smash them into tiny little pieces. Those people that you mentioned, all of them, they were all babies once. No-one is born bad. A person is a product of both nature and nurture, not just one or the other."

"I'm not an idiot. I know that. What's your point?"

"I'm the nurture, Mark. Me. I'm there getting them to embrace every dark thought; tip them over from thinking to doing. The thing you don't understand is how I'm there, whispering away, persuading cajoling – and believe me, some of them need very little of either of those. I told you earlier, I had nothing to do with Bin Laden or people like him. Bin Laden saw a world he didn't like; Tony Blair too. I had no input. Nothing. Nada. They acted because of the world and the way it is."

"Exactly," Mark said. "We don't need a Devil. Look at my face. Humans did this, not you."

"No, Mark, you misunderstand. This world, its current state, has been slowly created by me. Take the internet. My greatest achievement in centuries was persuading that Tim fella to give it away for free."

"Tim Berners-Lee is a great man. He did that for the good of mankind."

"No, he *thought* he did. Look at the trolls. The casual hypocrisy and misogyny. I don't even have to mention the homophobia and incitement of hatred. It's all there, everywhere. Even the kids, wasting their youth playing games online, actually giving more of a shit about whether they win than whether they've learnt something. You live in a world where being a You Tube star is actually a viable job prospect and you think the internet is *good*? Please, Mark, I expected better of you."

179

Elana reached out and grabbed Mark's hand, squeezed it tightly. He risked a look at her. She was pale, and sweat had stuck a couple of strands of hair to her forehead, but otherwise she looked fine. She opened her eyes wide at him and nodded. *Keep going.*

"Precisely. They need little encouragement. So why the need for you? You can't be everywhere at once."

"Ahh, Mark. Do you believe in God?" He didn't wait for an answer. "God is omnipresent, as well as being great and good and blah, blah, blah. He's everywhere, apparently. If He can do it, so can I. I was the greatest of his heavenly host once upon a time, you know, until he banished me. I'm not like you, I am not human. I have powers and desires you cannot possibly comprehend. Eight people dead tonight is 'small fry' compared to a tsunami or earthquake, I'll grant you that. But see, those natural things, they're nothing to do with me. They're not even anything to do with the big guy with the beard. That's the world, the Earth, just fucking with you, reminding you that you're not all powerful."

"I didn't talk about earthquakes-"

"No, you didn't. I did. I'm just getting the first strike in there, before your tiny little mind fixes on that. It's called a pre-emptive strike and some of your so called good guys have used it before. All the rapists and killers, they are like my bread and butter. They keep me going day to day. Think of it as like food for you: without them I can survive, but I'm not as strong. Now, things like tonight, this can keep me going for years."

"What? Why?"

"I've taken some normal people," he pointed at Bruce's corpse and then turned his finger to point at Mark with a smile, "and I've turned them into killers. Bang!" He clapped his hands together loud enough to make both Mark and Elana jump. "That's manna from heaven, man, mmm, mmm, mmm! If you'll pardon the expression, of course."

"You haven't turned me into a bad person," Mark muttered.

"No, Mark, I've turned you into a murderer. Tell me, before tonight would you have killed a man with a tire iron? Hit him repeatedly with it until he stopped breathing and his brains are all over the ground?"

Mark went pale at the memory.

"Now, anyone, in the right set of circumstances, could become a killer. Protecting a child for example, but you – you killed a man who was walking down a road."

"It wasn't like that."

180

"Already with the excuses Mark, well done." He breathed in deeply. "More power to me!"

"He was going to kill me."

"He wouldn't kill anyone," the giant said. "He was going to run away when them other two died. I thought he'd gone, but you killed him, did you?"

"Calm down, Simon." Adam said, holding a hand up. "Unfortunately, Mark, Simon here is right. Billy had decided that this wasn't for him and he wanted to go. This body was too weak at the time, because I would have stopped him. Already, you are doing my work for me, Mark."

Mark's mouth fell open. He wracked his memory. The three of them had been upstairs. He tried to think about what the monk – Billy - had been doing, but he couldn't remember. *What if he'd been waiting for the right moment? What if he was going to run as soon as they'd reached the other house?*

"No," he croaked.

"Yes," Adam said and this time all the monks joined in his laughter. "Now that - that gets me going. Good people doing bad things. Oh yeah, baby!" He licked his lips and made like he was swallowing something.

"What do you want from us?" Elana said.

"Do I have to keep going through this? I want you to spread the word: I'm here and I'm real. Simple really, bit like you."

"You're not going to kill us?"

"Now, why would I want to do that? Mark here is on his way to becoming a disciple and when he goes, it's only a matter of time before you follow."

"He will never follow you and neither will I."

"Brave words, Elana, but that's all they are."

"No, they are a fact. Tell him Mark."

Mark glowered at Adam. "Your words mean nothing. Your lies will not win you followers."

"My lies have done me pretty well so far."

"Getting Eve to eat an apple? Wow, good one."

"You believe that story?" Adam laughed. "You must be more simple minded than you look. God threw them out of Eden, not me, and it wasn't because they ate an apple. Read your bible again, there was another tree."

181

"Your lies get bigger, Adam. How can we be expected to believe that? Adam and Eve is the most ridiculous story out of all the ludicrous ones in the bible."

"The tree of life and the tree of knowledge." Adam laughed. "Everyone gets that wrong. God kicked them out because he didn't want them to live forever. He's a bastard like that." He waved his hand, dismissing the conversation.

"What now?" Mark said. "The police are on their way, what's your end game?"

"End game? You a chess player Mark? My end game is my business. Yours however-" He left the sentence hanging.

Mark looked around the room again. Monks were standing around them, effectively blocking all the exits. The door through to the kitchen and upstairs was nearest to them, and a monk leant on the bar near the door. The biggest one was standing behind Adam, his hulking form the only deterrent necessary for the front door. The other two stood off to his left, partially barring the view to Sandra's burnt corpse. *No way out here, no Bruce Willis heroics. What the hell am I going to do?*

He looked over at Elana and his breath caught in his throat. Her skin was so pale, her hair still stuck to her forehead, her lips devoid of any colour. He needed to give her a hug – hell, he needed to receive one. His eyes drifted to her stomach.

"Complete innocence," he muttered.

"What?" Elana looked wide eyed again. "Keep him talking!" she hissed.

"Is that your plan, Mark? Keep me talking?" Adam laughed.

"Not anymore," Mark said. "I don't give a shit about you."

Adam looked confused for a second, the first time his manner had become flustered.

"Get up, Elana."

"Stay where you are!" Adam barked.

"Trust me, babe. You can walk out of here, right now." He leaned towards her, taking both of her hands in his. "He can't hurt you."

"Try it, see exactly what I can do."

"I don't understand-" Elana started.

"Yeah you do, just think about it for a moment. He wants to corrupt us all, get us to spread the word or some bollocks like that."

She nodded. "But we're not going to do that. He's going to kill us." Her voice broke when she said 'kill'.

182

"No." Mark shook his head and smiled at her. "He can't kill you."

"Liar!" Adam roared.

"Think about the baby. Our baby."

Elana looked shocked for a moment, but then broke into her first genuine smile in hours. Mark turned back to Adam, watching the bigger man sink back to his chair.

"I'm right aren't I? You can't kill her because the complete innocent inside won't nourish you or whatever it is that killing does for you."

"Believe what you want. You can both die tonight."

"But not by you."

"There are others here."

Mark looked at each monk in turn, speaking slowly as he did so. "So, who wants to kill a pregnant woman?"

The monks all broke his stare; not one maintained eye contact with him. *Interesting, I'm on to something here.* He looked back to Adam and saw him shifting in his chair, trying to get comfortable.

Elana grabbed his arm again. "Can we go? Really?" She didn't sound right, didn't sound like her. It took him a second to realise why and he wasn't happy with the thought. Her voice was steeped in desperation.

"You can."

Her face fell. Her eyes widened, then a frown worried her brow, before her mouth dropped open and everything sagged. She even seemed to shrink against the chair. A sob escaped her lips and then she looked disgusted with herself. She drew herself together, almost visibly toughening up.

"No, Mark, I'm not leaving without you."

He was proud of her then, but frustration was a much bigger emotion. "You have to think about our baby."

"I am. I don't want him to grow up without a father."

"As touching as all this is, why don't you just shut the fuck up?" Adam snarled. "Don't underestimate me, Mark. You stand up, just see how far you get." He directed the last at Elana.

"Ignore him, babe. Get up and go."

"I'm not leaving you."

"It won't be for long. Just get yourself out, I'll be right behind you."

Elana looked between Mark and Adam and finally looked at each monk. She craned her neck to look at the one stood by the bar, nearest to the door to the kitchen. The monk looked away when she stared at him. She turned back to Mark, who was imploring her with his eyes.

"Just go," he said, "I'll be ok."

"No you won't," she said.

Mark saw something move behind the monks standing in front of the main entrance. A flash of colour, pale duck egg blue, gone now. He frowned and saw the tables and chairs behind the monks. *What was that?* Was something behind the table? Something out of sight of the monks? Were the police here already? It was too soon surely? They would not rush back would they? He wished he'd paid more attention to the many, many police programmes on TV.

He saw movement again, between the legs of the chairs. The monk behind them would surely see it soon. Maybe he was too high to see the movement. Mark didn't want to wait any longer to find out what the thing was. He guessed it had to be on their side, otherwise whatever it was would just have announced itself. He needed to distract the monks, to give them more time.

Time for his hero moment.

Saran slipped through the door, closing it silently behind her. A table and chairs had been pushed back into the space by the door. Two monks stood nearby, but both had their backs to her. She crouched down, hoping that the table and chairs would block the view of anyone else in the room. Adam's voice was soft but clear - which was impossible, he should be dead - but she ignored that. She peered through the table legs. Adam had his back to her and he was shaking with laughter. Just beyond him, Elana sat on a chair. She was a pale and drawn shadow of the beautiful woman who had walked into the pub hours before. Another voice cut across Adam's laughter. Mark! Everyone in the room seemed to be focussed on both Mark and Adam.

Just as well.

She held the shotgun awkwardly in her arms, cradling it like a mother holding a new born for the first time. It was heavy, the black metal shining in the dim light of the bar. She had been on protests before, screamed and shouted along with the mobs but the point of every single one of those marches was a dim and distant memory now; her

184

lifelong avoidance and abhorrence of violence being thrown into complete disarray by the evening's events.

Could I shoot a man?

Could she really? It would be easy – stand up, pull the trigger, pump the shotgun like they did in the films and pull the trigger again. Do that five times and the nightmare would be over.

Her hands were shaking.

She pictured it all happening, in slow motion, like a bad action film and she'd need a quip at the end. Something like "bar's closed" or "time gentlemen, please". The punchlines needed work. With these ridiculous thoughts in mind, she stood up, cocked the shotgun and held it at hip height.

Before her nerves could get the better of her, she pulled the trigger.

Mark realised it was Saran just before she stood up. "Run!" he yelled at Elana. She looked at him blankly before turning her gaze towards the main entrance just as a huge bang rang out. Blood showered out of the biggest monk, covering Adam as if someone had poured a tin of red blood over his head. Elana screamed.

Mark tried to get up, but it felt as though he were moving through treacle. Every action was taking so long. The monk to his right was moving towards him and Mark punched him, but the punch held the weight of a toddler's kiss. The monk hit him back, and Mark crashed to the floor. There was another loud bang, but Mark was on the floor, pain coursing through his head again. If his cheekbone wasn't broken previously, it surely was now. He could feel the swelling without touching it. He saw Elana getting up, still screaming, and moving towards him. She seemed a thousand miles away.

"No, run!" he shouted as loudly as he could. *Why isn't she listening?* It came out as a whisper. Another bang. His ears were ringing. Elana looked confused and he waved his hand towards the door. He looked towards the door and it took him a second to process what was going on.

"Run," he shouted again.

The first shot was so loud it made her jump. Mark was staring at her, open mouthed and the big monk turned towards her. Mark shouted something, but all sound in the room was muffled, like she had her head under a pillow. The monk's face didn't register surprise as the bullet tore into him; he had the same blank expression he had worn throughout the evening. The shot ripped right through his body, and the exit wound splashed gore over the back of Adam's head. Deep, dark red filled with small lumps of white bone, it was the most disgusting thing she had ever seen.

I did that. Everything still seemed distant. Everything was happening very slowly as if she had all the time in the world. A primal part of her acknowledged the raised heartbeat and roar of blood in her ears. A tiny voice was crying at the back of her mind: the part of her that was all that was left of the person who had never even hit someone before this evening.

She pumped the shotgun and fired again, this time at the other monk in front of her. She missed completely, the shot thudding into the wall on the other side of the bar. The monk dived to the floor, rolling towards the fire and taking shelter by the table there. He had rolled over Bruce's corpse.

He's dead then. She had known of course. From the moment he hadn't met her, she'd known he was dead. Grief overwhelmed her for a moment and tears rolled down her face. *Bruce, my Bruce.*

She saw Mark throw a weak punch at another monk and then get hit himself. He was in trouble that was obvious. For a big man, his punches lacked weight. Elana was moving towards him as he shouted something else and she was now standing still doing nothing.

"Run!" Mark shouted, and this time his voice was clear. Time seemed to be speeding up again; she was re-joining the normal world.

She pumped the shotgun and fired. The monk that hit Mark spun round and collapsed. Before she could move again, Adam was standing in front of her, pressing the barrel into his fleshy stomach and grinning through the blood on his face.

"Do it again!"

Saran pulled the trigger and nothing happened. Adam snatched it from her hands and threw it over his shoulder without looking. It clattered to the floor, sliding across to the bar. Adam grabbed Saran's head and twisted hard, snapping her neck. A whisper escaped her lips that might have been an attempt at a scream and then she sagged to the floor her life disappearing quicker than her bravado.

"No!" Elana screamed as Saran crumpled to the floor, her eyes wide open and fixed on her husband's corpse. Her features were slack now and her effervescent beauty gone forever. Elana ran towards the rear of the pub away from Adam. The monk standing there seemed dazed by what had happened, but as he saw her he started moving towards her. She saw his fist moments before it connected to her cheek and she fell to the floor. He aimed a kick at her ribs but she rolled away, hands wrapped around the warm barrel of the shotgun. As the monk stepped towards her, she roared and swung the shotgun like a baseball bat. The man had his mouth open in a snarl and the stock of the gun hit him on the side of his chin, breaking his jaw with an audible crack. He mumbled something and Elana swung the gun again as she stood. He spun around, teeth and blood flying out of his ruined jaw and then she held the gun above her head swinging it down like an axe. She raised it again and then felt a hand on her arm.

"He's gone," Mark said, gently prising the gun from her hands. She looked at him and nodded once. He cocked the gun and heard a round slip into the chamber.

"She's dead."

"Yes."

"She came back to save us and now-"

"Yes." He slipped an arm around her shoulders.

"What's he doing?"

Adam was standing with his back to them, head turned upwards. He was breathing in deeply, and appeared to be trembling slightly. Now he lowered his head and held his arms out. Mark looked around at all the dead in the room and felt sick.

"Feeding."

Elana felt bile rise and she had to spit it out. The acrid taste burned her throat and she fought more down. Adam was moaning now, the noise not dissimilar to orgasmic groans. She looked around the bar and the many corpses and shuddered. The whole room looked like the set of a horror film. Blood coated most of the walls, floor, seats and even the tops of tables. She had no idea where most of it had come from, and in truth she did not want to know.

"We should go," Mark said.

"Yes, god yes," Elana said.

Something about the room was niggling at her. Not the blood or gore. Not the charred remains of a woman she had found irritating whilst alive. Not the mad man drinking in the atmosphere of death and destruction. She looked around the room again, eyes resting on the bodies in turn but skating past Adam.

"Now, honey," Mark said, breaking her reverie. He closed his hand around hers and pulled her towards the door at the back of the bar. His other hand held the shotgun tightly enough for his knuckles to turn white. She followed, feeling light headed. *Something is wrong.*

They entered the kitchen, walking quickly now. The temperature dropped as the back door was wide open. Snow was gathered in the doorway, peaks and troughs highlighting how heavily trodden it all was. Mark didn't pause as he crossed the dried blood on the kitchen floor and that showed how far they'd come that evening. Their whole world, changed forever. Neither of them would have been able to walk through that much blood yesterday.

Snow crunched under foot and their breath misted the air in front of them. The hills rose in the distance, clearly illuminated by the big white moon. Stars twinkled above, so many more than they usually see.

"It's beautiful," Elana said, stopping for a second, mesmerised, despite everything.

"Yes," grunted Mark, dragging her forward. They walked into the narrow corridor between the ruined wood shed and the oil tanks. Darkness shrouded the end of the corridor; shadows caused by the hulking oil tanks. They heard a door bang behind them, loud and clear in the still night.

They both turned towards the noise and everything rushed back into perspective.

"He's coming!" Mark said. "Run." He stepped past her, back towards the pub, raising the gun to his shoulder.

"Mark-"

"Run, now!"

The monk stepped out of the shadows between the two boilers and she knew what had been wrong. The monk that had been next to them. The one who wasn't lying dead on the floor of the pub. The one who was now swinging an axe towards Mark's legs.

"NO!"

Mark flew up in the air as the axe smashed through his knees. Dark blood splashed out of his jeans and he landed with an 'oomph!' His right leg stuck out at an angle perpendicular to where it should have been. He was screaming, but somehow managed to raise the gun. The monk swung the axe again, above his head. Mark shot him. The gun worked this time, the bang echoing around the hills. The monk gurgled as his midriff opened, spilling his intestines over Mark's prone body. He sank to his knees then pitched forward, toppling like a spinning top. He landed on top of Mark and didn't move.

"Mark!"

"You need to go, babe," he said through gritted teeth.

"Not without you. Please, don't leave me."

Mark pushed at the body of the monk, but it didn't move. Tears ran down his cheeks. She ran to him and tried to pull the body. She reached under the arms and heaved, grunting with the effort. The body slid a little, but Mark was still stuck underneath.

"I can do this!"

Mark was very pale. He touched his leg and sharp pain coursed through his body. His hand came away sticky. He felt cold and for the first time that night he knew it wasn't to do with the snow. His entire right leg was numb and the cold was spreading through his body. The axe was lying next to him, his blood covering the head. The monk still had a tight grip on the handle. The shot had ripped up through his body, tearing through organs and shredding his heart, killing him instantly.

He looked at Elana who was still trying to drag the monk off him. Her face was red with effort and he felt despair at what was about to happen. He pictured her sitting with their son, reading to him. The son he would never know. He choked back tears. In the distance a door slammed, the bang echoing through the building and round the hills.

"Leave it, babe. You're running out of time."

"I can do this," she said again but it was no use. The monk was just too heavy and she was too tired. "Where are the fucking police?"

"On their way. Please, babe, go."

"I love you."

"I love you too. Tell him about me, but not this. Don't let him know about this."

"I love you, Mark."

"I don't think he can hurt you, but you need to go now."

She looked at him, tears streaming down her face. Fear wracked her body, by now as familiar a feeling as tiredness at the end of a long day. She was suddenly exhausted: all she wanted to do was lie down next to Mark and hug him until it was all over.

Another door slammed, this one almost as loud as the gunshot had been.

"Run. Don't stop and don't look back."

Elana knew she had to move then. She stood on shaky legs, kissed Mark hard on the lips then turned her back on him. She ran down the short gap and reached the fence. A gate barred her way. The lock was stiff but opened straight away and she was out, running onto the moor. She ran in a straight line, lifting her legs to clear the snow. Thigh burn kicked in almost immediately but she forced herself on, Mark's words echoing in her head.

Adam looked down at Mark with a grin on his face. The same borderline idiot grin he had worn for most of the night. The grin that had not once reached his eyes. Mark forced himself to grin back. His leg had gone completely numb and cold was spreading through his body. He could almost feel the pool of blood spreading underneath him. His breathing was shallow now, each breath rattling in his lungs.

This is it, game over man.

What film was that? Doesn't matter now.

"Hello, Mark."

"Adam."

"Quite a predicament you've found yourself in."

"Yeah. Bleeding a lot. Cold now."

"Never mind. You've not got long left."

"Didn't get your own way, did you?"

Adam shrugged. "Plenty more fish in the sea, as they say. I found followers easily enough and I wasn't even really here then."

"You couldn't hurt Elana could you? I was right."

He shrugged again. "I can hurt whoever I like Mark. Some people give me more than others. I'm looking forward to you."

Mark grinned again. *Keep him talking. Fucking easy really.* All the while, Elana was getting further away and the police were surely getting closer. *Who knew the Devil was such a boring, long-winded bastard?* He started to chuckle, then the laughs came. His leg throbbed with each laugh, and he was feeling weaker by the second.

"Game over, man." *Aliens, that was it. Great film. Never be able to watch that with my boy now.*

"For you Mark."

"And you."

Mark raised the shotgun. Adam laughed, shaking his head. "Come on, Mark, surely by now you've realised *that* can't hurt me?"

Mark nodded. "Of course, but then I got to thinking about that fire."

He shifted the barrel slightly. It was no longer pointed at Adam.

"Clever boy."

Mark pulled the trigger. The bullet tore into the oil tank. Mark saw the spark, felt the heat and that was that.

Elana heard the shot, felt heat at her back and then she was flying through the air. She landed hard enough for the wind to be knocked out of her. Seconds passed before she could roll over and look at the pub. Flames were gushing into the night sky. The room that was the kitchen was already on fire and the roof was catching now. Another explosion made her shield her eyes and the flames licked higher.

"Mark!" she screamed. "No! Mark!" She grasped her stomach. Tears coursed down her face and she sobbed his name again and again. Drawing her knees up to her chest, she sat on the snow rocking back and fore, watching the flames tear through the building. She could hear glass breaking and imagined the bottles of spirits and beer exploding, the alcohol feeding the flames further. It was warm where she sat, a feeling that, until now, had been utterly alien to her that night.

She watched the back of the pub, watching the burning gate, waiting. She chewed on her lip, anxiety gnawing at her insides. Something moved in the flames. Roughly man shaped, it stood in the midst of the fire, staring at her. She didn't – couldn't – move. Her breath froze in her throat. It took a step forward.

"No!" she cried.

Another step, although this seemed to take more effort. The burning man was dragging himself out of the fire. He raised a hand to point at her.

191

A fence post collapsed taking the burning gateway down with it and Elana shook her head. Nothing there after all. Had she imagined it? Shadows in the flames. She lay down in the snow, letting the heat of the fire warm her and closed her eyes. Exhaustion finally caught up with her. She closed her eyes, seeing Mark smiling at her, and passed out.

She didn't wake with the noise of the helicopters as they landed several hours later.

Author's note

There are many myths and legends about Dartmoor and I have used some of them in the writing of this book. Most of them are referred to exactly as the myths are told but some have been changed to suit the plot of this novel. Specifically, the tale of the gambler has been changed quite significantly. In the original myth, he is called Jan Reynolds and he was caught by the Devil in Widecombe-in-the-Moor. Jan was playing cards when he was taken by the Devil on horseback. As the Devil rode off with Jan, cards fell out of his sleeves and where the cards landed, you can still see the outline of the suits today. Maybe. If you squint a bit.

The pub itself is the Warren House Inn. It is the highest inn in Southern England and one of the loneliest. It does get cut off by snow and does indeed have a fire that has burned every day since 1845. I have no idea if the Devil has ever appeared there, and I have no intention of finding out.

Acknowledgements

As ever, this novel took more than just my efforts alone. My thanks go to the beta readers: Richard Evans and Shani White, who read VERY early drafts of this and were hugely encouraging about it; Katie Samuel, Jer Fisher, Chris Kenny, Vicky Browning and Tinú who all helped shape it for the better. Dan Beazley gave me good advice about the police, but any errors or inaccuracies there are mine and mine alone. John Germon 'translated' Adam's early speech into native Devonian, but I watered some of it down. There are still people who speak like that living down here and John gave his time for free and with great patience and for that I am very grateful.

Ric and Elaine Cooper first told me the legend of the Warren House Inn, and the cards on the hills around it, whilst walking on Dartmoor. I can't actually remember who told me the story of the gambler and the Devil (for the record, I think it was Elaine!), but it was whilst we were walking that the plot began to come to me.

Bruce Evans is a real person: in addition to being a good friend of mine, he also owns an excellent wine shop in Crediton (Grape and Grain): visit him carrying a copy of this book and you never know, he might give you a discount! Bruce paid for his daughter's name to appear in this book at an auction of promises in aid of Clic Sargent – a children's cancer charity. His generous donation means that his entire family appear in this: Elana, Tom and Saran.

Frank at GFIVEDESIGN came up trumps again with the cover, which features Janet Parsons and was taken by her husband Peter. At the time of writing, they are the owners of the Warren House Inn where this book is set. Go visit - eat some rabbit pie!

Finally, thanks as always to Tinú, Josh and Ethan for your patience whilst this was being written. I hope it lives up to expectations and no, Bear, you can't read it until you are (much) older.

Dave Watkins

April 2017

.

Printed in Great Britain
by Amazon

35954775R00112